Allegiance

Two Worlds Book #3

By Timothy L. Cerepaka

An Annulus Publishing Book

Annulus Publishing, Cherokee, Texas, 2015

Published by Annulus Publishing

Copyright © Timothy L. Cerepaka 2015. All rights reserved.

Formatting by Timothy L. Cerepaka

Contact: timothy@timothylcerepaka.com

Cover design by Elaina Lee of For the Muse Design

(http://www.forthemusedesign.com/)

ISBN-13: 978-0692553602

ISBN-10: 0692553606

Acknowledgments

I would like to thank my uncle, James Wilhite, for helping me get this manuscript into publishable shape. I'd also like to thank the rest of my family for supporting me while I wrote this novel. You guys rock.

Chapter One

With a hood cloaking mine face, I walked with a quickened pace through the streets of mine tiny and quaint hometown, Old Ways, located in Northern Se-Dela, far to the south of most major bustling cities and towns in this part of the country. It had been six years since I last stepped foot in this town and I had never intended to return here again, but the Mission required that I do so and I dared not go against the Mission, no matter how uncomfortable its requirements may at times be.

'Twas a quiet little town, Old Ways was. Of course, it was early morning, with the crisp cold morning air and the sun beginning to rise in the distance. Still, when I glanced up at the sky, I could see the prison of the Old Gods, also known as the moon, fading out of view. I prayed a quick prayer to the Old Gods to grant me the strength I would need for what I am about to do.

As the morning was still young, I saw no other people as I walked through the village. None of the villagers were awake; even the animals slept. I spotted an old guard dog slumbering deeply on the front porch of a house, the creature not stirring even one inch when I passed it by. It had a bone 'tween its paws and might have been dreaming of wide open fields and playful children, though I knew not for sure, because I was not a dog.

I, too, dreamed of things. I dreamed of the day when the worlds would be one again. Dreamed of the day when the endless bickering and fighting among the peoples of Dela and Xeeo would cease. Dreamed of the day when the Mission would be complete and I and mine fellow Reunification members could rest at long last.

Most important of all, I dreamed of the day when mine siblings and me would be reunited, when we would put behind ourselves the petty arguments and silly disagreements that had ruined our relationships betwixt ourselves. As the mansion in which I grew up loomed closer and closer in mine vision, I was about to make that particular dream of mine a reality.

The mansion up ahead—tall, foreboding, and seemingly empty, although I knew that it still had within it at least one inhabitant—towered over every other hut in the village. Whereas most of the little houses here were tiny, with perhaps two or three rooms at most for a family of three or four, this mansion had three stories, with several balconies upon which I had spent many summer days as a youth sitting on, watching the prison of the Old Gods rise in the distance as day became night or playing games like flip coin with mine siblings when our parents had expressly forbid us not to.

Even so, I fingered the handle of the skyras sword sheathed at mine side. I normally was not one to use Xeeonite technology of any sort, for 'twas unnatural and unwieldy in comparison to Delanian magic and equipment. Still, mine beautiful sister Kiriah had insisted I bring this blade along with me in case I should need to defend myself, although I saw no reason for it, seeing as I was not here to fight anyone.

ALLEGIANCE

Nonetheless, I allowed Kiriah to give me one such weapon, for after so many years apart I did not wish to ruin our brief time back together by denying her one of her requests. Besides, it reminded me of the sword I once wielded as a Knight of Se-Dela, although unlike that silver blade, this one was much lighter and allegedly superior due to its laser blade. Having not yet had a chance to test that theory, I knew not whether that was true; perhaps I would train with the sword after I completed this mission.

Soon I was climbing up the steep, narrow dirt road leading from the village up to the mansion. 'Twas not a terribly difficult climb, to be sure, as I had gone through much worse since leaving this place long ago (although due to a bout of amnesia afflicting me, I could barely remember most of it). With the sun rising in the east, I saw more and more of mine old mansion the closer I approached it.

It appeared to have been well-taken care of, for the windows reflected the rising rays of the sun as sparkling as ever, while its blue coat of paint looked as fresh as a woman's powdered nose. Most of the upper windows were shuttered, although that was clearly due to the fact that it was once night time, for even the shutters looked as beautiful as ever.

Also, the front gate—with its replica of the full moon attached on top—looked the same as it always did. A tall wrought iron fence surrounded the mansion on every side. It brought back the sweetest of childhood memories, that fence did, such as the time that mine brother and I attempted to climb over the fence when we were younglings, only for us to fall due to the sleekness of the bars. That had been the most painful day of mine young life, yet I

3

now look upon the memory as fondly as a mother looks upon her children.

But despite how well-taken care of this place looked, I dread approaching it. For I did not only have sweet childhood memories associated with mine home; nay, I had more recent memories, the kind that I did not wish to remember, which left a sour taste on mine tongue and left my soul blacker than the heart of an arctic vampire.

Memories of fear, searching for my missing sister … memories of anger, arguing with my brother, even punching him in the face, which 'twas a terrible memory I worked to forget, though I never truly did … and memories of shame, memories of stomping out of that mansion and vowing never to return to this place or gaze upon the face of mine brother again.

But here I was now, striding up to the wrought iron fence, up the same path I had walked up and down on from the earliest days I could walk. The Old Gods could be humorous at times, setting aside our fates to go against our own vows. 'Twas probably the reason why mine parents always warned my siblings and I against making rash vows to the Old Gods, for they would be certain to test the truthfulness of those statements that we made in the heat of passion and anger.

I expected the gate to be locked, which would not be much of an issue as I could open it even without a key. Yet when I approached it and pressed my fingers against the cold metal, the gate swung open silently and without resistance.

This did make me hesitate. My brother, Sura, who as far as I knew still lived here, never left the gate unlocked before. This did make no sense to me. Sura was as predictable as a clock, always locking the gate when the last vestiges of the sun set and always opening it when the first rays of the sun peeked over the horizon in the early morn.

Granted, the sun was indeed rising, yet this gate did not appear to have been unlocked and opened by my brother. Nay, I noticed the lock lying on the pathway, smashed off by some unknown force. This did leave me uneasy and afraid; nonetheless, I pushed the gate open entirely and stepped within the fenced area.

The front yard of the mansion looked as well-kept as the rest of mine old home. The square bushes, planted by my father even before I was born (Sura had been but a year old when they were planted), stood against the house 'neath the front windows on the first floor. The grass was trim and cut, with nary a place for any enemies or predators to hide from me.

On the right side of the yard was the full moon-shaped birdbath, which was as dry as the Dead Lands, another alarming sign to me, because brother Sura loved the tiny red wings and the sometimes large skiplegs that often came for a drink and a bath. Why would mine brother ever forget to refill the birdbath? Did make no sense to me, especially when I noticed how well-kept the rest of this place was.

The left side of the yard had the headstone of our parents, a beautifully-crafted piece of masonry again shaped like the moon when it was full in the sky. I saw nothing strange about it at first until I noticed … nay, that could not be …

I walked up to the headstone, ignoring the text written upon it, mine eyes focusing squarely on what I thought at first was an illusion, but which now I cannot deny. Just above the name of my father—FARIL, carved in large block letters—was the tiniest chipped area.

I took notice of this aberration—nay, this crime against my parents' memory—because Sura had always taken care of this headstone with great pride. Every day, after his morning duties, brother Sura would go out to this headstone and painstakingly clean it, brushing out each carved letter and washing away the grime and dust which gathered upon its surface. He would even cover it with three thick woolen blankets when it hailed so as to prevent it from being damaged.

This terrible sign confirmed what I feared: Something had happened to mine brother, something that had prevented him from doing his usual duties. It had to have happened very recently, perhaps as recent as last night, for the rest of the mansion still appeared in good shape.

Hence, I drew mine skyras sword from my belt. 'Twas currently inactive, but I felt the tab I could press to make it flare to life, which I rested my thumb upon so I could use it in a pinch. I hoped to the Old Gods that I would not need to, that maybe brother Sura had been stricken with some illness that had left him bedridden, but this seemed not to me like that was the case.

Advancing toward the front door of the house, mine eyes flicker to the shuttered windows. Perhaps they were not shuttered so as to protect mine brother's privacy, but instead were shuttered to hide the evil villain who had dared to harm him. Who this was, and why they did this, I knew not; however, mine instincts told me that this must still be here, and therefore I could not let mine guard down for even a moment.

The front door of the mansion 'twas one of the few things on the house which brought me no early memories, for the old door had been replaced by a new door after it had been destroyed due to an accident I no longer recalled (although it must have been humorous, for even in this grim situation, it nearly brought a smile to mine face).

The front door looked not broken open, but I knew, from a brief alliance with a thief sometime ago, that there were ways to pick a door's lock without it appearing that it was so. When I wrapped my hand around the smooth wooden doorknob and turned it without effort, I knew someone had indeed picked it.

Yet I had no choice but to go inside if I wished to find out what happened to my brother, so I pushed the door inwards, still holding mine skyras sword at mine side. 'Twas prepared to fight to the death if necessary, for no one was allowed to harm any member of mine family, even family members I am on no good terms with.

When I opened the door, I was greeted by a familiar sickening smell: The stink of the popular drug known as super speed, which smells like smoke and mud. I recognize the stink because I was once a dealer of the super speed drug between the time I left home and the time I became a Knight of Se-Dela. 'Tis a stink ye never forget, for there is an addictive quality to it even to those such as myself, who never became addicted to the drug which we sold to the poor souls who devoured it like candy.

This alarmed me greatly, for brother Sura never used super speed drugs. As a priest of the Old Gods, Sura was forbidden to use any sort of drug that might affect his clear mind and good judgment. Did seem unlikely to me that my brother would ever even allow a user into this mansion, even if that user were a homeless and wounded traveler with no family with which to stay.

The entryway was almost pitch black, though I caught a whiff of a nearby candle that had been put out somewhat recently. Still, I did not need light to find mine way around, for I knew this mansion like the back of mine hand. I knew that to my right 'twas a wooden rack, built by our father years ago, for our shoes, under mine feet was a carpet meant to catch the mud and dirt on the soles of my shoes, and a coat rack was to my left opposite the shoe rack. I also knew that directly ahead of me was the foyer, with the stairs leading up and up to the upper floors and doors along the hall that led to other rooms.

Yet I hesitated, my hand still upon the doorknob, mine eyes scanning the shadows for even the tiniest hint of danger. The light from the sun outside illuminated the entryway enough to show me that there was no one waiting in hiding to kill me. Even so, the mansion was eerily quiet, even for Sura, who while not as boisterous as I, still made much more sound than was present in this place.

Should I leave? Or call for help? Kiriah had given me a messenger device, which currently was in my left pocket, to use to contact nearby Reunification members in case of an emergency. 'Twas a useless little thing, for I despised most Xeeonite tech, but as with mine skyras sword, I had taken it because Kiriah had insisted I take it.

On the other hand, however, I did not need think I needed aid. While Sura's disappearance was troubling, I saw no sign to suggest that many beings have invaded our home. At most, three villains may have ambushed my brother in his home, and I was more than capable of handling three villains on my own, no matter how tough they may be.

So I gently closed the door behind me, without saying a word, and then advanced slowly toward the stairs. Mine instincts suggested that Sura was likely in his room on the second floor, which was usually where he breakfasted. Besides, I did not smell the scent of cream and bread that my brother usually ate for breakfast every morning. All I smelt was the stink of super speed, which made me all the more eager to reunite with mine brother.

With every step I took, I fully expected to be attacked by whomever had come here, although nothing emerged from the darkness to injure me. It occurred to me that it was possible that whoever had assaulted mine brother was already long gone, but that did not seem likely to me. If that were so, I would have heard Sura calling for help or demanding to know who had entered his house.

Nay; whoever had assaulted mine brother was still here. Perhaps they were not on the first floor, but that did not mean I had the luxury of letting my guard down. My foes likely expected me to walk in as mindless as a toad, though they underestimated mine intelligence and tenacity for sure.

Whenever I passed a door, I would press mine ear against its surface and listen as closely as I could. Every time, I heard nothing at all on the other side of the door, which made this action of mine seem fruitless, although I continued to do it anyway just to be thorough.

Soon, however, it became abundantly clear to me that this first floor was abandoned. I was the only being down here, no doubt, which meant that I would need to climb the stairs to the upper floors in order to find my brother.

As silently as I could (though 'twas likely a fruitless gesture, seeing as my foes above probably already knew I was here), I climbed the stairs, which creaked not under my weight, for these stairs were sturdy and had withstood the pressure of three rambunctious young children for three full decades without breaking. Like with the rest of this mansion, I had fond memories of these stairs, but I could not focus on them at the moment, for I could not afford to be distracted when there was danger in this house.

After every step, I paused for a brief second to listen for the sounds of anyone above. I heard nothing, which did not reassure me much at all. Nay, it succeeded only in increasing my anxiety and tension, for I was now beginning to wonder if Sura were alive at all. I wished Kiriah were with me; as my sister, she always knew how to calm my fears, although I knew that as the Leader of Reunification, she had many important issues to deal with while I was away and therefore could not come with me even to see our older brother again.

Soon, I reached the top of the stairs, which opened out onto the second floor hall. 'Twas slightly lighter up here than it was done there; a handful of tiny candles, which smelled like blueberries, lit the area, although not enough for me to tell if any adversaries of mine lurked within the shadows.

Then I heard a loud *thump* and I immediately jumped. I also pressed the tab on the handle of my skyras sword, causing its blade made of skyras energy to extend into existence. I looked around hurriedly, but saw nothing that could have made that sudden *thump*. Although it at least confirmed that I was not alone in this mansion, that there was someone—or, the Old Gods forbid, some*thing*—in here with me.

The glow of my skyras sword revealed to me a little more than the candles did. Opposite me was the self-portrait of mine father, Faril, wearing his pure white priest robes of the Old Gods, while carrying the Divine Books within his arms. He looked young in this portrait, which made sense, seeing as this had been painted years ago, when I was only a small child, but even so, his gentle black eyes looked the same as when I was grew older. Mine own mother, in fact, always used to say that my father's eyes never aged, which I now understood for perhaps the first time in my life.

But again, I returned mine attention back to my surroundings. I decided to check the second floor, seeing as that *thump* I heard earlier seemed to come from somewhere around here. Where, of course, I knew not, but I was prepared to fight if the villains who hid in the shadows should dare to show their ugly faces.

Hence, I went down the hall, in the direction I heard the *thump* come from, mine skyras sword at my side and glowing, which I decided to keep active in case the villains who had broken into mine brother's house were awaiting me in ambush.

I made my way down the hall slowly but surely, listening for any sound that would tip me off to the presence of my enemies. Unfortunately, I heard not a sound aside from mine own breathing and mine heart beating away inside mine chest, sounds which sometimes seemed to fill mine ears like an exploding cannon ball.

Then I heard another sound, one that did not come from mine own body. 'Twas the sound of someone's weight shifting, as if they had been standing in place for too many hours. Did sound like it came from a door on the right side of the hall, only a few feet ahead of me. The sound ceased quickly enough, but I made my way up to the door because I knew that that was where it came from.

I placed mine hand on the handle, but did not turn it immediately. Instead, I listened closely, as closely as I could, for any other sound on the other side. I knew not, after all, who might be waiting behind this door, whether he be friend or foe, although like before, I heard nothing at all.

Still, I could not afford to turn and leave, not so soon, so I took a deep breath, made certain that I was holding mine sword as tightly as possible, and then turned the knob and entered.

This room was well-lit in comparison to the rest of the mansion. Light from several candles illuminated the room, their combined light so bright that I had to blink several times to allow my eyes to adjust to the change in brightness. When they did, mine heart nearly failed me by what I saw.

There, on the other side of the room, sat mine brother Sura, his arms and legs bound tightly to the wooden chair he sat upon. His head rested upon his chest, making it impossible for me to see his face, although his long brown hair was messy and torn in a few places, which worried me greatly.

Brother Sura was not alone, however. Standing around him were a dozen of the deadliest-looking criminals I had ever seen in mine life. They were a motley crew—some elves, some dwarves, others human—but a fearsome crew nonetheless, for each member had one red skyras ring on his index finger, rings which identified them as belonging to the Red Ring Smugglers.

I raised mine skyras sword, but then someone from behind

who I could not see pushed me forward. Startled, I staggered forward in an attempt to catch my balance, but as I did so, I heard the door slam shut behind me. When I regained my balance, I looked over mine shoulder and saw that the door was closed and likely locked as well. This meant I had no avenue of escape, for there was no other way out of this room save for that door.

Yet I did not allow this to panic me, even though internally I cursed these criminals to the Old Gods for their treachery. Instead, I held my skyras sword close, in the way Sir Lockfried trained me to wield mine weapon in the face of numerous enemies, as I turned to face the Smugglers again.

"Foul criminals," I said, making no effort to hide the hatred and distaste in my voice. "Unhand my brother, or be prepared to live the rest of your rotten lives without your index fingers."

One of the smugglers stepped forward. 'Twas an elfish woman, with long blonde hair done in elven braids and a short elven blade sheathed at her side, but despite her beauty, I knew her well enough to see the evil lurking within her pitiless soul.

"Apakerec," said the elvish woman, flashing a smile at me, although I knew she was not happy to see me. "Long time, no see."

I gritted my teeth, for I remembered well this wicked woman and was not fooled by her friendly tone of voice. "I wish it had been longer, Orelia."

She did not look much offended by my words, although when she spoke, she placed her hands over her heart and put on a show of pain. "I am hurt. You and I used to be so close when you were a Smuggler. Don't you remember? I even recruited you into the organization."

"On the basis that ye could help me find my long lost sister, ye wench," I snapped. "Which, I will remind thee, ye failed to do. All ye had me do was break the law and operate under the cloak of secrecy in order to keep the Knights of Se-Dela from arresting ye, which they had every right to do."

Orelia's hands fell to her side and a sneer appeared on her face. "Right. I forgot how stupid you sound when you talk. You sound like you just walked out of an ancient storybook."

"I speak the High Tongue of mine forefathers," I replied, "which I have inherited along with mine brother and sister."

"The High Tongue." Orelia laughed. "I notice how you use 'my' sometimes instead of 'mine.' Not very consistent, are you?"

"'Tis due to the influence of outsiders like ye," I said, somewhat shamefully. "Otherwise, I would speak a more perfect version of the High Tongue."

"Sure," said Orelia with a smirk. "Anyway, I am happy to see you, Apakerec. No deception here. After all, if you hadn't come here today, all of this planning and taking your brother hostage would have been for naught."

Mine eyes flickered over to Sura, who still had not moved so much as one inch in his seat. He was so still that I almost feared that he was dead, although when I noticed his chest rising up and down slightly, I was reassured that he was in fact alive.

"Why did ye attack my brother?" I asked, returning my attention to Orelia. "He has nothing to do with ye. He is a noble priest of the Old Gods. Attacking a priest of the Old Gods is a grievous offense for which swift justice must be performed in order to correct it."

Orelia smirked. "You didn't sound so defensive of your

brother when you told me about him. In fact, you were quite angry about him, if I recall correctly. Angry enough to say awful things about him that you probably would not want repeated to his face."

"I was angry," I said. "I meant none of it. Even if I did, that gives ye no right to break into my brother's house and hold him hostage on his own property. 'Tis a wicked thing, but I suppose I should not be shocked, knowing how terrible ye Smugglers are."

Orelia folded her arms across her chest. "We only roughed him up a little. Want to see his face?"

Before I could respond, Orelia snapped her fingers. One of the Smugglers—likely a new member, for I did not recognize his face —grabbed Sura's hair and jerked his head up. I grimaced upon seeing his face.

Sura's face normally looked somewhat like mine, albeit with a stronger jaw and a wider forehead. Now, however, it looked like beaten meat, with dried blood covering much that was not already split open. His nose was broken and his left eye was swollen shut. A drip of some liquid that I could not identify from a distance leaked from his nose and fell onto his lap. He did not appear to be conscious, for he failed to show any signs of recognition in his eyes when his head was raised.

"Sura," I said. I glared at Orelia. "What did ye do to him?"

"Just roughed him up a bit is all," said Orelia with a smile. "Because Noman hasn't forgotten you, Apakerec, or how you used your knowledge of us to help the Knights of Se-Dela ruin our operations in this region."

I hesitated when she mentioned Duka Noman, the leader of the Red Ring Smugglers. 'Twas a dangerous man—not as

15

dangerous as some, but dangerous enough that it was usually unwise to anger him. I had not expected to hear from him ever again after I joined the Knights of Se-Dela, although I perhaps should have expected he would send someone after me at some point. I simply did not expect him to send someone after Sura, however, which was the most vile and wicked thing that Noman had done to me.

"And I do not regret it," I said. "Ye must have known I was never a loyal member of your petty little criminal gang. My allegiance has always been to the Old Gods, first, and to my family, second."

"Noman doesn't really care," said Orelia, shaking her head. "He told me he wants you dead. So excuse me if I don't show much interest in your principles and goals."

"But that is why I left the Smugglers and became a Knight," I said. "The Knights of Se-Dela offered me hard evidence of the location of mine sister, evidence ye Smugglers failed to give me. Though I imagine ye must know that already, as Noman is quite the well-informed man, is he not?"

"He is," said Orelia. "About the only thing he *doesn't* know is where you've been for the past two and a half weeks. Even our contacts within the Order of the Knights of Se-Dela didn't know where you were."

I bit my lower lip. Two and a half weeks ago I had gone to Xeeo in search of my sister … and found not only her, but a new purpose for mine life, as well. 'Twas why I had left the Order of the Knights of Se-Dela, for there was no way that the Knights would ever understand what we at Reunification were attempting to do.

"Ye need not know of the reasons for my absence," I said, putting on a brave face so that they would not sense any weakness from me. "'Twas private business."

Orelia shrugged. "Noman doesn't really care. All he cares about is the fact that you've gone a full year now without getting killed, even though that's what a dirty traitor like you deserves."

"Yes, I did indeed find it strange how ye avoided me when I was a Knight," I said. "Why was that?"

"Because the Red Ring Smugglers can't just waltz on in and kill any Knights we want to, obviously, even with our contacts in the Order," said Orelia. Then she leaned forward. "I noticed you said '*was* a Knight.' Are you not a Knight any longer? Who are you working for now?"

"'Tis none of your business, she-elf," I said. "Or Noman's, for that matter."

Rage burned in Orelia's eyes like a blazing inferno, but then she pulled back and returned standing upright. "Fine, fine. As I said, Noman doesn't care and neither do I. The point is that we have you where we want you, which is to say, alone and unable to escape from this place."

I looked around me. I had not noticed, but as we spoke, Orelia's fellow Smugglers had been surrounding me. Some stood by the sofa, others by the bookshelves, but none of then left any openings for me through which I could escape. Even the door was blocked off by a large human man, who looked like he might have been part dwarf if his bulk meant anything.

All the while, the stink of super speed filled my nostrils, though as far as I could tell, none of these Smugglers were on the drug right now. 'Twas a tragedy; not because I liked the drug, but their staying off the drug made them much harder for me to fight.

"I still do not see why ye dragged my brother into this," I said, addressing Orelia again. "He had nothing to do with my bad mistakes, which is often what I think of ye Smugglers as. 'Tis a great injustice to beat him so."

"Because we knew you would come back to see your brother sooner or later," said Orelia. She gestured at the man holding Sura's head up, who let Sura's head fall down back onto his chest. "We originally came here because we thought your brother might know where you went, but then we decided to make ourselves at home and wait here until you decided to come by and visit him."

"Ye knew of mine … testy relationship with mine brother," I said. "How did ye know I would ever come back?"

"We didn't," Orelia admitted. "It was more of a coincidence, really. While we were interrogating your brother, our lookout came in and said he saw you coming up to the mansion. We all hurried to hide in here so we could work together to get you when you arrived."

"I see," I said. "A devious trick of yours, though I am not shocked, for I have come to expect such deception from ye."

"Good to know you still remember us," said Orelia. "For a while there, I was starting to think that you had forgotten all about us. Glad to see that my fears were misplaced."

"It matters not whether I remember ye or whether I forget ye," I said. I nodded at my skyras sword, the heat of its blade rolling over mine face. "I will chop down each and every one of ye and then place your heads on the fence outside as a warning to all who would dare to harm my family."

"You certainly sound serious enough to do all of that," said

Orelia. "Unfortunately for you, Noman said that we're not supposed to let you have a fair fight."

She snapped her fingers again, and the man who had grabbed Sura's head now drew a long, serrated knife from his leather holster. He then placed the knife's blade under Sura's chin, close enough that he could slit mine brother's throat if he so desired.

"You have two options," said Orelia. She held up two fingers. "One, you fight us, and we kill your brother in cold blood. We don't really have anything against him, but we know how much you care about him, so holding him hostage is quite logical, wouldn't you say?"

I gritted my teeth. "What is mine other option, wench?"

"Option number two," said Orelia. A terrible smile came over her lips. "You drop that dangerous-looking skyras sword of yours and let us tear you apart piece by piece. I would have said you should also not scream, but I know I can't really expect that from you, so I'll take what I can get."

"Vile villains," I snapped. "Monsters, the whole lot of ye. Cursed from your mother's wombs, never to—"

"Does that mean you're going with option number one?" said Orelia, interrupting me as abruptly as if I had not been talking at all. "That's what it sounds like to me. I mean, it's your choice, but that really doesn't seem like a good choice to me, at least if you give a damn about your brother's life anyway."

I held my tongue, even though I had a thousand other curses I wished to hurl at these foul criminals. But I knew from experience that the Red Ring Smugglers were not the kind of monsters to make idle threats that they failed to follow up on. Nay, the Smugglers always killed who they said they would kill. 'Twas why I always worried about them coming after me when I was a Knight of Se-Dela. Now it was clear that I should have been worrying about Sura, who was infinitely less capable of defending himself than I was of defending myself.

"Nay," I said. "I will not be going with the first option. I spoke rashly earlier."

"Option number two, then?" said Orelia. "It would be a lot more sacrificial, you know, maybe even sweet in its own way, although we elves tend to think sacrificing your life for someone else is pretty silly. Still, I know how you humans think, so I was just looking at it from your point of view."

I had forgotten how much Orelia rambled. 'Twas as annoying as a pebble in the heel of my boot, but I did not allow her rambling to distract me. For Orelia was a cunning she-elf, second only to Noman in the Red Ring Smugglers, and to let mine guard down around her for even a second was to invite death upon myself.

But I could not go with either option. I did not want Sura to die, despite our estrangement, yet I did not want to die, either, for I had a grand Mission ahead of me that I could not abandon. I wished to reunite Sura with my sister and I, and I could not do that if I were dead.

Yet, as I noted earlier, I knew that I could not count on the Smugglers bluffing. If I fought back, they would kill Sura without thinking twice about it. Even if I managed to defeat them all, Sura would still be dead. 'Twould be a pyrrhic victory, if even that.

"We're waiting for your answer, Apakerec," said Orelia. She glanced at the Smuggler holding the knife to mine brother's neck. "Or would you like us to choose for you? Personally I think option number one would be the best, as that would rid us of both of you, but—"

"I am thinking," I snapped. "Please, give me a few more minutes in which to think this over. Can ye grant me that much, at least?"

"Well … fine," said Orelia. "But only three minutes. Noman doesn't want us wasting time here, not when there are a lot of super speed shipments that need to be sent out and other enemies of his that need to be killed."

Three minutes 'twas hardly enough time for me to come up with a way out of this, but it was more than I thought she would give me, so I intended to make every second of that time count.

I looked around the room in which I stood, looking for anything that could help me discover a third way out of this predicament. Sadly, all I saw was the Smugglers surrounding me on every side, looking eager to kill me, even though I knew not one of them personally. Still, the Smugglers were a rotten bunch and took any sort of betrayal as a personal slight against them, even if the traitor in question was not intending for it to be personal.

If only there was something I could do … anything … but nay. It appeared as though I was indeed caught in a tangle, unable to escape with mine life. The Founder of Reunification would be terribly angry if I were to die, but what else was I to do? Let these beasts kill mine brother? Nay, 'twas an unthinkable idea.

Seeing as I could not think of any way out of this situation alive, I pressed the tab on mine skyras sword again, making its energy blade retract into it. I placed the weapon at mine feet and kicked it toward Orelia in order to show the Smugglers that I truly had no plans to fight back.

"Very well," I said, looking at Orelia with as much hate as I could muster, for it was all I could do now. "Ye can have me. Just spare mine brother."

"The Red Ring Smugglers always keep their word, Apakerec," said Orelia as mine skyras sword stopped at her feet. She snapped her fingers again. "Men, why don't you give Apakerec a concrete display of the Smugglers' 'no quitting' policy?"

Her fellow Smugglers did not even wait for her to finish speaking before they began to advance on me. I would have picked up mine sword and fought them all off if I had had my sword, but I did not. All I could do was stand there and hope that I would die under the first blow, as I did not wish to remain aware of the sheer pain I was likely to experience when they took mine life.

The Smugglers carried chains, knives, even swords, and more than a few had brass knuckles that turned their fists into the deadliest of weapons. Though all of them were different species, 'twas obvious how each one was looking forward to giving me the beating they believed I deserved for my crimes against them.

I lowered mine head and closed mine eyes. Still I could hear them approaching, smell the stink of super speed wafting off their bodies and breath, listen as they grunted in pleasure at the thought of killing me. I prayed a quick prayer to the Old Gods to grant me protection from the Smugglers, though I knew better than to expect it.

At that moment, however, the floor shook under mine feet. 'Twas a subtle movement, one I barely felt, but there was no mistaking it. However, I continued to think that it might have simply been the combined weight and movement of the Smugglers somehow making the floor shake when I remembered that the floors of this mansion were extremely stable and could handle far more weight than this before they would so much as stir.

Then the floor shook again and I opened mine eyes and raised mine head. I was still surrounded on all sides by the Smugglers, yet they had all stopped now and were looking around the dimly lit room in confusion. Even Orelia was looked as if she was not certain what was happening, which told me that this was no trick of the Smugglers.

"What was that?" said Orelia, the tips of her ears twitching, a sign that she was losing her cool. "An earthquake?"

"Nay," I said, shaking my head. "Northern Se-Dela has not suffered an earthquake in well over three centuries. I know not what this is."

The floor shook once more, this time so violently that I was nearly thrown off my feet. Some of the Smugglers lost their footing and fell on their behinds, while Orelia staggered over to the nearest desk and leaned against it for support. Sura, meanwhile, moved not an inch in his chair, even though a shake as violent as that should most certainly have toppled his seat.

"Must be a trick," said another Smuggler, the one in front of me. He pointed at me accusingly. "He grew up here, didn't he? I bet he's doing something to make the mansion shake so he can scare us."

"Foul villain, I am just as ignorant of the true nature of this development as ye are," I said in annoyance. "Ye give me more credit than I would ever even give to mine self."

"He's lying," said the Smuggler. He raised his knife at me, an evil smile spreading across his lips. "And I know the best way to make this stop: Kill him!"

The Smuggler leaped toward me with frightening speed, his knife coming directly for mine throat. He leaped too fast for me to react, but even if I could, I would not have been able to stop his assault, for I was unarmed and helpless.

But as it turned out, I did not need to defend myself, for a large shadowy hand launched down from the ceiling and snatched the Smuggler before he could harm me. The Smuggler had only a moment to cry out in alarm before the hand pulled him back up into the ceiling, where he vanished into the shadows.

'Twas such an unexpected action that the rest of the Smugglers stood back, fear covering each of their faces. One of the Smugglers even turned and ran for the door, but another shadowy hand shot out from the threshold, grabbed him, and dragged him into the shadows kicking and screaming. His screaming was cut off the minute he vanished in the darkness and we saw no more of him.

"What the hell is this wizardry?" said Orelia. Her cool facade had dropped away completely now; her eyes were wide, her ears twitching so fast that they were almost a blur. She had drawn her own weapon now, an elven blade, but she still resembled a frightened kitten more than a fearsome criminal. "What is this? I don't—"

Another shadow hand extended from the ceiling and grabbed at her, but Orelia slashed at it with her sword. Unfortunately for her, however, her gesture was quite meaningless, for her sword cut through the hand harmlessly, allowing the shadow hand to grab her blade and yank it out of her hands. The shadow hand immediately retracted into the ceiling, taking her shining elven sword with it.

That did seem to be the last straw for many of her fellow Smugglers, for they dropped their weapons and ran to the walls screaming in horror. They did beat their fists and feet against the walls and door, making such racket that I could barely hear myself think. One Smuggler, a dwarf, even tried to hide under the sofa, although he was too fat and succeeded only in hiding his head under it; 'twas a useless gesture, for another shadow hand shot down from the ceiling and yanked him into the darkness before he could utter even one more word.

Orelia dashed up to me and grabbed the collar of my cloak. She brought my face up to hers, allowing me to see her pale face and smell the stink of super speed on her breath. Her eyes were slightly bloodshot, a common symptom of overuse of super speed.

"What's going on here?" Orelia demanded. "Is this some kind of trick? What are you doing?"

"She-elf, in all of the days I have lived here, I have never known my mansion could do anything like this," I said.

Another shadow hand shot down from the ceiling and grabbed one of the Smugglers by the leg. The Smuggler screamed so loudly that mine ears hurt before he was dragged upwards into the ceiling, where his scream was cut off as abruptly as that of the last screaming Smuggler who had been dragged into the darkness.

Orelia let go of my collar and pushed me back. She stepped back, fear crossing her elvish features, as she said, "Your brother must know what's going on here."

She turned and dashed over to my brother before I could say another word. Sura was still unconscious and still, but now it seemed more terrifying than sad, for I did not understand how he could remain thus in the midst of all of this chaos.

Orelia stopped in front of my brother and raised his head with one hand. She then slapped him so viciously that blood shot from his face onto the floor, which made me feel quite ill indeed.

"Wake up," Orelia demanded, her tone becoming increasingly hysterical. "Wake up, you bastard. What's going on here? Tell me!"

Over Orelia's shoulder, I saw Sura's non-swollen eye flicker open. He blinked it several times, but rather than look around this place in fear and confusion, he smiled.

"Ye ask me what is going on here, heretic?" said Sura. Even I did not find his smile very calming. "The judgment of the Old Gods, of course."

"What does that even mean?" said Orelia. She raised her hand to slap him again. "I'm not even going to ask. You're clearly behind it, so I'm going to kill—"

Yet another shadow hand shot down from the ceiling and grabbed her by her raised hand. Orelia looked at it in shock, but before she could say anything, the shadow hand yanked her up toward the ceiling, where she vanished as silently as a dying wind.

She was not the only one to disappear. More and more shadow hands appeared, grabbing the remaining Smugglers and dragging them into the darkness. Most of the remaining Smugglers struggled against the shadow hands; indeed, I would have said that their struggles were almost noble or perhaps tragic if I did not utterly loathe all of them with my very being. Good riddance, I say.

Within a few minutes, all of the Smugglers were gone. The only hints that these villains had been here at all were the dropped weapons and the strong stink of super speed, although as all of the Smugglers were no longer here, even that stink was not quite as terrible as it once was.

I stood there for a full minute, expecting the hands to return and take me, even though I now knew that Sura was indeed behind them. Yet the hands did not return and the darkness appeared as normal as ever.

Lowering my hands, I dashed over to Sura, whose head had flopped onto his chest again. I stopped briefly to pick up my skyras sword, then resumed running over to him. Pressing the tab on my sword's handle to extend the energy blade, I quickly and easily cut the ropes tying him down, which stood not a chance against the heat of my blade.

Once all of the ropes were undone, they fell to the floor. Sura also leaned forward and likely would have fallen with his ropes had I not caught him in time, holding one hand on his chest. I felt his heart beating, though not as heartily as before, and felt his lungs breathing, though again, 'twas much weaker than it normally was.

I pushed Sura back up to a sitting position. Deactivating mine skyras sword, I placed the hilt back in my robe pocket and gently lifted up Sura's face. His one good eye opened again, focusing on my face with sheer incomprehension. I saw black lines retreating from his face down his neck and under his shirt, but I understood not what those meant. His skin, too, appeared pale, like he was sickly, though whether that was due to the injuries he had sustained from the Smugglers or whether it was due to those mysterious shadow hands, I knew not.

"Brother," I said. "Do ye recognize me? It is I, Rii, your younger brother."

"Rii?" said Sura, his voice weak. Another smile crossed his lips. "Oh, Rii, how long has it been since I last saw your face? Ye remind me of our father. 'Twas so long ago that he died. So long ago."

"I know," I said. "Let me help ye. I know not exactly what those monsters did to ye, but I will do what I can to heal ye. Do ye want me to call the village healer?"

"N-Nay," said Sura, shaking his head slightly. "I … ye can heal me yourself. 'Tis a healing kit in the—"

"In the kitchen," I finished. "Yea, brother, I remember. I will go get it as soon as I get ye to your bed. Ye need rest."

"Th-Thank ye, brother," said Sura. He sounded close to fainting. "But before ye do that, I have one last thing to share with ye."

"What is that, Sura?" I asked.

Sura coughed out some blood, which alarmed me greatly, before saying, "Those Smugglers will never bother us again."

He said that like it was a great joke, for he smiled and chuckled after those words left his mouth.

Then his eye closed and the last of the black lines on his neck vanished. I could tell he had lost consciousness again, which meant I would need to get him back to his bed with haste.

Picking him up in my arms, I walked toward the door as

quickly as I could, trying not to think about the horrific screams of the Smugglers as they were dragged in the darkness. I also tried to ignore the lingering stink of super speed, although I did not succeed very well in that endeavor.

Chapter Two

I brought mine brother to his room, which was just across the hall. After putting him in his bed, I made my way down to the kitchen on the first floor, which was still dark due to the closed shutters. It was not quite as tense as when I first arrived, however, because I knew there were no more Smugglers hiding in the shadows, although I still remembered those hands, which hardly made me feel much better.

I found the healing kit in the top pantry of the kitchen, where it had been kept for as long as I could remember, filled a cup with water in case Sura was thirsty, and then returned to my brother, who was still resting in his bed. It took me only a minute to apply the healing cream and bandages on his face that he needed, although his face was so badly wounded that I believed he would need superior medical attention if his face was going to heal correctly.

After applying the cream and bandages to his face, I placed the cup of water on the stand next to his bed and then sat on a nearby stool and watched him sleep. I considered waking him, but after everything he had been through in the past day or so, I decided that he needed rest more than he needed to talk to me; this despite my overwhelming curiosity to find out what had happened to him and how he had summoned those dark hands from before. I also wished to know the fates of the Smugglers, although if what mine brother said was true, then I could already guess their untimely fates.

As I sat there, I looked around Sura's room. It had at one point been mine parents' room, but when they died, Sura had moved into it. 'Twas a large room, with a walk-in closet on the other end of the room that, as a child, I had always liked to pretend was a cave of sorts, where vile monsters that I needed to slay awaited. Nowadays, Sura kept his clothes in there, although simply looking at its closed door brought a grand smile to my face as I remembered the old days.

The bed Sura laid on was queen-sized, which was because mine parents had shared this bed with each other for as long as they were alive. The blanket was made of a soft red silk, while the fluffy pillows upon which Sura rested his head held goose feathers within them. This bed, too, brought back memories from when I was a child. Mine parents would let me crawl onto the bed with them when I became afraid of some nightmare I had, which made me feel as though nothing could harm me. I always told myself, however, that it was really I who was protecting them; at least, that is what I would tell my parents when they asked why I wished to sleep with them, and they would never question it.

A massive oak dresser stood on the other side of the room, opposite me. It had a large mirror, in which I could see my and Sura's reflections. That dresser had a dozen drawers, some big, some small, although I had little memories associated with it, for as a child that dresser had never been as fun as the walk-in closet, although I recall mine father once telling me that that dresser had once belonged to his father, which made it very old indeed.

The blue curtains were closed, but I could see through them the faintest light of the morning sun. I considered getting up and opening them to allow more light to pour in, but I decided against it, for I did not want to risk being spotted by anyone outside. 'Twas too much of a risk, even though we were on the second floor and at the back of the room, where no one could see us.

At that moment, the back of my head ached with the pain of a thousand hammer swings. I grabbed the back of mine head, gritting my teeth from the sheer pain, although having spent so much time feeling this pain already, it did not bother me as much as it once did.

This head pain had plagued me ever since I joined Reunification two weeks ago. Kiriah had told me that it 'twas merely the side effect of the machine, called the Brain Editor, used to heal mine injuries, for prior to joining the organization, I had been mortally wounded in battle against someone and had needed medical assistance quickly to save me.

Who I had fought, why they had fought me, I remembered not. Mine memories of the time between my journey to Xeeo in search of Kiriah and mine joining Reunification were misty, at best, which Kiriah informed me was yet another side effect of the machine that healed me. I sometimes tried to remember what had happened, but all I ever recalled was an awful stink in my nostrils like garbage and sewage, so I generally focused on the present.

Besides, 'twas hardly a thing worth worrying about. What mattered more than anything was completing the Mission. Whilst it would have been nice to remember those memories, I knew they were not important to the Mission; therefore, I did not mourn their loss. Nor did I have a strong desire to ask Kiriah or any of the others about how I ended up in that way; 'twas unnecessary.

Mine thoughts were interrupted when Sura moaned. I started, almost knocking mine stool over, although when I realized that it had only been my brother's moaning, I calmed down.

With all of the bandages covering his face, mine brother more resembled one of the wrapped corpses of the Kukanes Desert than a living and breathing human being. His one good eye flickered open and he turned his head to look at me, although that seemed to be the only part of his body that he could move in his current condition.

"Brother?" said Sura, his voice still quite weak. "I am thirsty …"

I grabbed the cup of water on his nightstand and brought it to his lips. "Drink, brother, as much as ye need. If ye need more, simply say so and I will dash down to the kitchen as fast as Zaunas's lightning."

Sura drank slowly, no doubt due to the pain in his body. Then he waved his right hand, which I took as a sign that he was done. I pulled the cup from his lips, although to my displeasure some of the water fell onto his blankets. Thankfully, 'twas nothing more than a few drops, although I still loathed it, for I despised getting water on our furniture.

"Thank ye, brother," said Sura, whose voice now sounded much stronger than before. "I know not what I would have done without ye. Likely, I would have perished and gone to be with our parents and the Old Gods in paradise."

"Let us thank the Old Gods, then, that your reunion with our parents is still some ways off," I said. I placed the half-drunken cup of water on the nightstand. "Brother, do ye suffer from any other injuries I know not of?"

"N-Nay," Sura said with a cough, though thankfully he did not cough out any blood this time. "Most of mine injuries were to my face. None of my bones were broken, though those sinners threatened to break every bone in my body for my refusal to aid them in finding ye."

I tightened my grip on my knees. "Those monsters did not even realize that ye knew not where I was. What villains."

Sura chuckled again, that same chuckle from before. "Curse not those who seek to harm us, younger brother, for only the Old Gods may place curses upon them. Though knowing their fates now, a curse from the Old Gods would likely be an improvement over their current situations."

As before, Sura laughed. I laughed not with him, for even though I despised those Smugglers as much as he (if not more so, for I knew them better than he did), I found his laughter off-putting. It didst not seem natural for mine brother, who I had never known to laugh at the plight of our enemies.

Sura's laughter lasted only a few seconds, however, because 'twas interrupted by a terrible cough that made me fear that he had been wrong in his assessment of his health. His cough left just as quickly as it came, however, leaving Sura lying still on his bed, a smile on his split lips.

"I see," I said. "Well, brother, it is a good thing I came when I did. It must have been the Old Gods guiding me back to our mansion so I could save your life, although it seems to me that mine presence here is unnecessary with those shadow hands that dealt with the Smugglers."

"No, no," said Sura, shaking his head slightly. "I am glad ye are here, brother. Without ye, I would not have found the strength to call upon those hands. I believe, along with ye, that the Old Gods did indeed lead ye here, even if ye did not know it at first."

I nodded. "I agree. Yet that does not explain what those hands were. Whilst I am as glad as the sun that they saved us, I do not recall ever seeing those hands in this mansion before; nay, I do not even recall knowing about them. Can ye explain what they were to me?"

Sura did not answer immediately. Perhaps he was thinking about my question or maybe he was too tired and worn out from the beating he had received from the Smugglers to answer. I understood that well, although that did nothing to calm down my curiosity, which was as powerful as the rays of the sun on a hot summer's day.

Finally, Sura looked away from me, which I found infuriating, although in character for my brother, who was usually not the most forthright person in the world. "Why do ye not first tell me about why you have returned home? I thought ye would never come back. When I heard that ye joined the Knights of Se-Dela, I thought ye had truly abandoned the Old Gods in favor of Waran-Una."

"I joined them only because the Knights promised to help me locate Kiriah," I said. "Never once did it occur to me to worship that fool of a king. Mine loyalty lay always with the Old Gods and with the teachings of our ancestors, even though I often dispensed justice in the name of Waran-Una."

"I understand," said Sura, though he still did not look at me. "I suppose the Knights of Se-Dela are better than the Red Ring Smugglers, who I also heard that ye were working with."

"But no more," I said. "No more do I work for either the Knights of Se-Dela or the Red Ring Smugglers. I find both organizations contemptible now; yea, I have nothing to do with either."

"Then who do ye work for?" said Sura. He looked at me, this time with a questioning gaze. "Ye have told me nothing about your new employers, whoever they may be. Are they yet another criminal gang, perhaps one on Xeeo?"

I shook mine head. "Nay, brother. I have renounced organized crime. The organization I work with now is the noblest organization in all of the two worlds. There is no better group of beings anywhere."

"What might this organization's name be?" said Sura. "'Tis the Delanian Bounty Hunter Alliance, mayhaps?"

"Nay," I said. I looked around, even though 'twas no one in here to listen, and then leaned in a little closer. "They are a secret group, one which operates in the shadows, but fear not, for their goals are noble. Ye have probably never heard of them, not even whispers of their actions."

"Brother," said Sura in a warning tone. "Ye know how I feel about those who operate in secret. 'Tis untrustworthy, as the Divine Books say."

I rolled mine eyes. "Yea, I know how ye feel, but I cannot help but find it might hypocritical, seeing as ye have operated as a priest of the Old Gods in secrecy for many years to avoid notice by King Waran-Una."

"I do it only for our own safety, brother," said Sura. He then raised his left hand and pointed it toward the door. "Now, unless ye wish to leave the room, let us return to the subject at hand:

Why did ye return? Did ye fail to find Kiriah and so decided to make amends with me for our past falling out?"

"I did not fail to find Kiriah," I said. A smile broke over my lips, a smile I was unable to control. "Indeed, brother, 'twas the opposite: I found her."

Sura nigh jumped off his bed in shock, but his injuries kept him on his mattress. Still, it did make his bandages move around slightly, which meant that they were not as secure as I had thought I had made them. I reached for them, but Sura was already readjusting the bandages himself; thus, I lowered my hands to my lap.

"Ye must be joking," said Sura as he finished readjusting his bandages. The disbelief in his one good eye was obvious. "Kiriah has been missing for six years. How can ye have found her? We have had no clue as to her whereabouts. Indeed, for a long time, I thought her dead, which is why I did not join ye in searching for her."

"'Tis true," I said. "And I can offer you undeniable proof of our reunion as well."

I reached into mine pockets and felt around until my fingers found the glossy, square photographs I needed. I then drew the three photographs from mine pockets and glanced at them briefly. Each one showed me and Kiriah standing together, arms around our shoulders, smiling at the camera. Kiriah, with her blonde hair and small nose, looked a little different from me, but our familial resemblance 'twas obvious even to those who knew us not.

I handed the photographs to Sura, who took them and brought all three up to his face. His good eye widened considerably and tears began to flow from it and his swollen eye, tears I had never seen before, for I had never known Sura to cry about anything. The only time I recalled seeing Sura sad enough to cry was at our parents' funeral; even then, he still shed no tears for them.

"I … I believe ye, brother," said Sura, his eye locked on those photographs as if they were the only thing in the universe. "The woman in these photographs 'tis be a little older than the Kiriah I knew, but there is no denying that she is one and the same."

"Indeed, brother," I said, my own voice almost choking with emotion, despite the fact that I had been reunited with Kiriah for some time now. "We took those pictures before I returned here. Her personality is still much the same as well. And she wants us to be with her again. Both of us."

Sura tore his eye away from the photographs and looked at me in surprise. "Where is she? What is she doing? How far is she from this place? Can ye take me to her?"

I held up mine hands to slow down the flood of questions washing over me. "Hold, dear brother, for I was just about to answer your questions."

Lowering the photographs, Sura said, "Then answer them, brother. And leave out no fact, no matter how small; I know ye well enough to know that ye are not always the most honest of individuals."

That jab came out of nowhere, but I ignored it, for Sura always treated me like this, at least since Kiriah's disappearance. Part of me hoped that maybe Sura would have dropped his negative feelings toward me when he saw those photographs, but mine older brother could be quite the stubborn ass when he wanted, so I perhaps should not have expected differently from him.

"Kiriah is on Xeeo," I said. "She has been living there for the past six years. Do not worry; she is perfectly fine. In fact, I would say that she is better than ever, because she and I are working together to complete a grand Mission the likes of which the worlds have never known."

Sura tilted his head to the side. "Whilst I am glad to hear that Kiriah is doing well, I must admit to being mystified by your talk of a grand 'Mission' that ye two are working toward. What may that be?"

"It is another reason I came here to talk to you, brother," I said. "For ye see, Kiriah and I now work together in the same organization, the organization that I mentioned earlier. I did not work with her at first, but eventually I saw the light and now wish to share that light with ye."

"Are ye now going to tell me what this organization is called?" said Sura. "Or are ye going to keep me guessing in the dark?"

"The organization is known as Reunification," I said. "But do not tell anyone that. We operate in the shadows, where few know of us, and we prefer it that way."

"I suppose that is why I have never heard of Reunification," said Sura, nodding. "Though I admit I am somewhat skeptical of this organization, if they truly work in the shadows as ye say; still, perhaps they are not so bad if both ye and Kiriah are working for them."

"Indeed, they are quite noble" I said. I looked toward the ceiling, imagining the greatness of the Founder and our Mission. "Our Mission is grand, yet most individuals on both worlds would be against it if they knew, for knowledge does not always come with understanding."

"What, then, is your 'Mission'?" asked Sura. "I notice that ye still have not answered that question."

"Our Mission is simple," I said. "We are working toward reuniting Dela and Xeeo, which were once one world so many years ago, but were separated due to a massive catastrophe of the highest order. We will bring them together and restore the harmony that 'twas lost in the chaos of separation."

I expected Sura to shake his head and say that that was a silly thing. After all, the vast majority of the inhabitants of both Dela and Xeeo believed that the two worlds had always been separate. 'Twas a lie, of course, one taught and propagated as fact throughout the ages, but a lie was still a lie even if everyone believed in it.

Much to mine surprise, however, Sura did not look surprised or skeptical of that claim at all. Indeed, he stroked his bandaged chin, as if deeply considering the implications of that fact.

"'Tis an interesting idea," said Sura, "though not the first I have heard of it. The Divine Books say that the Old Gods emerged from the chaos that preceded Dela's creation, a chaos oft-described as the separation of two worlds. Yet the Divine Books always said that both of these worlds were lost in the chaos and that Dela had been created by the Old Gods to replace them."

"I have never heard of that story," I said. "Why did ye not mention it to me until now?"

"Because 'twas always an obscure story," said Sura. "And besides, ye never showed much interest in studying the Divine Books, especially in your younger years. Though if ye had, ye would have known already."

ALLEGIANCE

Mine hands balled into fists on my lap, but I decided not to push the subject. Sura could be like this, I reminded myself. As father's successor to the post of priest of the Old Gods, Sura had an encyclopaedic knowledge of the Divine Books. Certainly, Kiriah and I had read the Books in our younger years and could quote some verses by heart, but our understanding paled in comparison to Sura's, which he always boasted about, especially when we were younger. His arrogance always bothered me, but again, I had to ignore it, for I was not interested in getting into an argument with him at the moment.

"Anyway," Sura continued, "I did not know it was even possible to reunite Dela and Xeeo. Of course, I also did not think that the two worlds were in any way related, although I suppose they are if ye say they are."

"It is indeed possible," I said, nodding. "The Founder, who created our organization, has decreed it possible. We have agents on both Dela and Xeeo working toward completing this glorious Mission. And we are very close to achieving our goal; soon, both worlds will be one again."

"How?" said Sura. "How can they be reunited? Even if it is possible to reunite them, would that not require the power of the Old Gods to accomplish? Yet the Old Gods are in the moon, locked away and unable to aid ye in accomplishing that goal even if they would like to help."

"I know not how the Founder intends to accomplish it, but rest assured that he has it figured out already," I said. "Soon, our worlds will be one again and the Mission will finally be completed. The pain of separation will no longer bring grief to the peoples of the two worlds."

Sura, however, stroked his chin again, a frown on his face. He said, "Whilst I understand that ye are looking forward to this, I cannot help but wonder about the deaths this might cause. The Divine Books described the chaos of separation as a horrible thing in which millions of people died. 'Twas so horrible that the Old Gods created the sky to hide its terror from Dela's inhabitants, so that we would avoid losing our sanity and be able to build a new society without fear. Would not a reunification of the worlds cause similar chaos and destruction?"

"Ye do not understand," I said. "Separation brings death. Unification brings life. 'Tis what the Founder and the Elders believe and 'tis what I believe as well."

"Ye make these platitudes and statements, ye offer no evidence to prove them to me," said Sura, in his usual irritating, matter-of-fact tone he used whenever I said something he did not agree with or find very believable. "I cannot imagine that reuniting Dela and Xeeo would be a peaceful thing. Whilst separation does sometimes cause chaos, the Divine Books also state that forcing things together can cause just as much damage if done hastily and without thought."

"The Founder does not act hastily and without thought," I snapped. "He is a great man, better than you or I will ever be. I find it humorous that ye judge him when ye have not even met him."

"I judge not those I have not met," said Sura. "I only point out the potential problems in your grand 'Mission,' as ye call it. Though perhaps my worry is for naught; maybe this 'Founder' individual has already come up with a way to avoid creating yet another catastrophe."

"He has," I said. "I am certain of it. Now, brother, will ye join us? That is why I came here in the first place, after all. Kiriah asked me to recruit you to our cause. That way, not only will our family be reunited at last, but we will also be able to work together to achieve a Mission far greater than any of our individual lives."

"An interesting offer," said Sura. "Of that, there is no doubt."

"'Tis not just an interesting offer, brother, but the *best* offer," I said. "Ye do not understand how great this Mission is, how wonderful this opportunity to work with us is. This grand future belongs to all and it is our job to bring it about, as the Founder says. And we can do it together, as a family at long last."

Sura stroked his chin again. He seemed to be thinking deeply about mine offer, which was good, because I wanted him to. Although in truth, I would have been happier if he had simply accepted the plan immediately, for then my family would have been reunited at last and life could go back to the way it was before Kiriah's disappearance.

"I would indeed like to be reunited with our sister," said Sura. He looked at the photographs again. "It has been too long since I last saw her. If this will give me the opportunity to be with her again, then it does seem logical to me to accept your offer."

I put mine hands together in eagerness. "That is wonderful to hear, dear brother. Once ye are rested, I—"

"But sadly, I fear that I will have to decline the offer for now," said Sura. He smiled at me in an apologetic way. "Sorry, brother."

I stared at Sura. "Wait … ye are declining? But why? Do ye not want to be reunited with Kiriah? Do ye not want our family to be one again?"

"I would indeed love to see my sister again, after so many years apart," said Sura, nodding. "But I am not certain that I want much anything to do with your Reunification group, for they do not seem to have much fealty to the Old Gods. And it is my duty, as a priest of the Old Gods, to stay here and continue the legacy of our ancestors."

"But …" I struggled to find the words to say. "But ye can still be a priest of the Old Gods *and* be a member of Reunification. The two roles are not mutually exclusive, after all."

"Be that as it may, mine younger brother, I still prefer to stay here and preside over our family's legacy, than to leave and aid an organization I know little about," said Sura. "This does not mean that I cannot meet Kiriah again, however. Why not have her visit me here? I think our reunion would be much more greater if done here, in the privacy of our home, than in Xeeo or some other place like that."

I rubbed mine forehead, quite unable to believe what I was hearing. "I … But …"

Sura reached out with his left hand and patted my forearm. "'Tis fine, brother. I am simply glad to know that ye and Kiriah are still alive. I prayed to the Old Gods day and night for your safety, even when I did not feel very kindly toward either of you. It appears that my prayers were answered."

I still did not know what to say. I ran a hand through my hair as I thought about what I could say to make him come with me, but no answer came to mind. For I did not think I could come up with a good response to answer his arguments, seeing as Sura was quite the stubborn mule and rarely budged when he made a decision of any sort, even if that decision was unwise or foolish.

"Thank ye for coming to save me from those Smugglers," said Sura. "Whilst I ultimately dealt with them myself, it was your appearance that gave me the courage to stop them once and for all."

"Is that why ye did not summon those ... those odd shadow hands until I arrived?" I said. "Could ye have used them at any point?"

"I did not use them initially because I was unconscious for some time there," said Sura. "That, and they would have killed me if they had noticed me summoning them. You distracted the Smugglers for me, which allowed me to take them out, as ye witnessed earlier."

"Ye still have not explained what those hands were, brother," I said. "Seeing as I have already explained what Reunification is, I think it only fair that ye share your secrets with me."

As before, Sura looked away. He seemed mightily ashamed of those hands, which puzzled me, as he had not seemed so ashamed of them when he summoned them earlier to smite those Smugglers. It made me wonder what kind of changes had happened here since Kiriah's disappearance. Though I was not going to drop the point; perhaps while we spoke, I would be able to come up with a clever counter to his reasons for declining to join Reunification. 'Twould give me more time to think of some way to convince him to join us, anyway.

"Yea, I know how strange those shadow hands looked," said Sura. "They are indeed odd things, but they are not evil. At least, I do not believe they are."

"That does not sound much certain to me, brother," I said. "But please continue."

Sura sighed, like he did not wish to continue to speak, but then he said, "After Kiriah's disappearance and ye and I had our disagreements and went our separate ways, I threw myself into studying the Divine Books. 'Twas to distract me, ye see, for I did not wish to dwell deeply on our fractured family."

I nodded. "Yea, I understand."

Still not making eye contact with me, Sura said, "Not only that, but I fasted for a week. I prayed to the Old Gods day and night, paying little attention to my own needs and wants. I even neglected to take care of the mansion, beyond ensuring that there were no major holes in the roof or that anything needed major repairs."

That sounded like mine brother. Sura could be quite hard on himself in the middle of a stressful situation. Still, I found it amazing that he apparently became so interested in his studies that he neglected the mansion, as my brother was always meticulous about keeping the family house in good shape.

"I felt no connection to the Old Gods at all during that time," said Sura. He sounded close to tears. "None whatsoever. It was the darkest period of mine life since the day our parents died. For a brief time, I even considered taking my own life."

That alarmed me. It had never occurred to me that Sura might have been this close to ending his own life. He had always seemed stronger than either me or Kiriah. I felt like a wicked brother for not bothering to inquire about his health at all during those six years we were separate.

"But then I received a vision from the Old Gods," said Sura. He rubbed his right cheek, though that did seem like an unconscious move to me. "'Twas the strangest and scariest vision

46

of mine life. In it, I saw our parents kneeling before the Altar of Judgment, where all spirits go when they die. They were receiving judgment for the way they lived their lives, though whether I was seeing an actual event or a symbolic hallucination, I know not even to this day."

I well recalled reading about the Altar of Judgment as a child. 'Twas a scary thing, for it was said to be where every good and bad deed of your life was put on display as a sacrifice to the Old Gods. If the Old Gods accepted your sacrifice, then ye would go on and rest in peace; if not, ye were damned to the eternal fires below, where all villains burned for the rest of their lives.

"What happened to our parents in that vision?" I asked. "Were they granted the eternal rest that they earned?"

Sura's lips trembled, but he continued speaking as normally as ever. "Our parents did put their good deeds and their wicked deeds on the Altar, with great trembling. And the Old Gods did smell their sacrifice and decided that it was good."

I sighed in relief. "Oh, how happy I am to hear that! I thought for certain that ye were going to say that the Old Gods rejected their sacrifice."

"I am not yet finished with mine story," said Sura, who did not sound happy despite the news. "Thus, I saw our parents drawn up into the Gods' Abode, to rest forever, as they deserved."

"I do not understand why ye sound so unhappy, brother," I said. "Is it not glorious that our parents now rest in peace? 'Tis a wonderful thing."

"Indeed, and that thought does make me happy," said Sura. He tried to smile, but failed. "But that is not where mine vision ended. Nay, that is but where it started."

"What did ye see after that?" I asked.

"What I saw, I do not know for sure," Sura said. "Dark hands reaching out to me from the darkness, trying to drag me away into the shadows. I heard voices clamoring for me to join them, heard the Old Gods whispering among themselves about things I understood not, and witnessed the devastation of a land—full of beautiful green fields—that I had never known. 'Twas extremely traumatizing."

"What does it all mean, brother?" I asked, leaning forward toward him. "It all sounds exceedingly cryptic and vague."

"I do not know," Sura admitted. "It all happened so fast and I had so little time to understand it. The vision ended as quickly as it came and I found myself lying on the floor of this very room, sweating as profusely as if I had spent all day working in the Fertile Plains on a hot summer day."

"What happened then?" I said. "What did ye do?"

"Nothing," Sura said. He gestured toward the center of the room, where a round blue carpet lay. "For a day and a half, I lay there on that carpet, thinking about that vision. I did not get up even to use the bathroom, though to be honest, I do not recall ever needing to use it. My hunger, however, grew painfully strong, and it is my hunger that eventually drove me to stand up and leave."

"Is that it, then?" I said. "Did ye go and grab a quick snack to sate your hunger after that?"

Sura finally looked at me. His one good eye looked mournful and serious. "'Tis when I discovered that I can use those hands of shadow that I used earlier. When I was in the kitchen preparing something to eat, I saw movement in the shadows out of the corner of my eye."

He shuddered. "At first, I thought it might be a mouse, for I had been finding more and more of those rodents in the mansion ever since our parents died. Yet when I went to investigate, I found nothing in that darkened corner of the kitchen, so I returned to making mine meal when I saw movement again."

Sura looked around when he said that, like he expected a monster to come flying out of the shadows as he told me his story. I saw nothing out of the ordinary in this room, but with Sura acting so nervously, I also began to feel worried that we perhaps were not as alone as I thought.

"I slept not for three days after that," said Sura with a shudder. "And when I tried to rest, I made certain to light as many candles as I could in order to keep the shadows away. Even so, I still saw the shadow hands from the corner of mine eye, always vanishing like the mist when I turned to look at them."

"Sounds like a terrible thing," I said. "A truly frightening phenomena. What happened next?"

Sura brushed some of his hair off his forehead. "Eventually, I began to believe I was going mad, that my fasting and lack of sleep was starting to take hold of my sanity. It did indeed make me weary and afraid, even to the point where I believed that the Old Gods were afflicting me with this horror for reasons I could not understand."

Sura sounded as lost and terrified as a little child now, which made me feel exceedingly sorry for him. Still, I continued to think of ways to convince him to join Reunification, although I also tried to listen at the same time.

"It was a month later that this nightmarish event ended," Sura said. He patted the blankets of his bed. "'Twas lying here, in mine bed, trying to sleep, when one of the shadow hands fell from the ceiling and snatched me like a cat catches a mouse. I was pulled upwards into the shadows, kicking and screaming, but the hand did not let me go, nor did it acknowledge mine terror. I am not certain that it can."

Sura shuddered again. "And what I saw in that endless darkness was ... I cannot even describe it, younger brother. Things slithered in the shadows, grunts and roars bombarded mine ears, but it all ended soon enough and then I found myself lying in mine bed again, doubting whether what I had experienced had been real, a dream, or something in betwixt."

"And after that?" I said.

Oddly, Sura smiled at me. His smile seemed to hide a little bit of fear behind it, though I was so put off by his grin that I said nothing about it.

"I discovered I had control of the shadow hands," said Sura. He raised his normal hands and turned them over. "I could summon them from wherever the shadows dwell. They can grab anything and drag it into the darkness. I have learned that it is impossible for anyone to escape from these hands when they grab hold of ye."

"But how is that possible?" I said. I glanced at mine brother's naked fingers. "Ye do not have skyras rings, and ye know as little about magic as Kiriah and I."

"I understand it not, either," said Sura. "I have had this ability for six years now. Originally, I tried to ignore it, for it terrified me greatly; but eventually, I made peace with my new powers. Now I view it as a part of me, as essential as mine normal hands, and which I must accept as well as any other part of me."

ALLEGIANCE

Sura's smile contrasted sharply with his resigned tone. I began to believe that mine older brother might be suffering from a lack of sanity, although I chose not to say that aloud so as not to anger him.

"What happens, then, to the people that your shadow hands drags into the darkness?" I asked. "Such as those vile Smugglers. Are they still alive?"

Sura's smile never wavered. "I know not for certain where they are, although I suspect they went to the place I went to: A dark world, full of terror and monsters. If they survive, I doubt it will be with their sanity intact."

I had to repress a shudder. Whilst I was no fan of the Red Ring Smugglers, especially after how they treated mine older brother, I did think that this punishment might have been too much even for them. Would have been better, perhaps, if Sura had instead defeated the Smugglers and summoned the Knights to take them away to be tried and jailed for their crimes. Although I was thankful that he had not done that, for I did not wish to see the Knights again, not when they were searching for me to find out why I had not returned to duty.

Deciding to turn mine thoughts to happier matters, I asked, "What happened to Hajan? I lost touch with him after Kiriah's disappearance on that night."

Sura's smile vanished in an instant. "He died a year ago. 'Twas a freak accident; he was riding his horse when it was spooked by a flame rat and it threw him off its back. He landed on his head and broke his skull open against the road. I presided over the service at his funeral."

I put a hand over my mouth. Hajan had been a family friend

of ours; indeed, I could not remember a time in mine life when the middle-aged, red-haired man had not been with us. He had been mine father's best friend, but had grown close to all of us as we aged. I had always thought of him as an uncle of some sort, even though I lost contact with him just as I had with Sura over the years.

"That is terrible," I said. "Was there no way to save him?"

"There were no doctors or healers nearby at the time, and even if there were, 'twould have been fruitless, for he had died upon impact with the road," said Sura with a sigh.

"I wish I could have been at the funeral," I said. "But I heard very little news from this village when I was a Knight, so I had assumed that Hajan was still alive."

"That is fine, brother," said Sura. "Hajan did not go to his grave bearing grudges against you or anyone else. 'Twas a peaceful man, which is what made his death so sad and tragic."

Despite Sura's assurances, I found it hard to remain happy and upbeat. Perhaps mine presence would not have been enough to save Hajan, but I should have at least attended the funeral, if nothing else.

But then I swiftly banished that thought from my mind. Whilst Hajan's death was tragic, he was no member of Reunification; therefore, being upset about his death would only get in mine way. That was what the Founder would have said, I was certain, although that did not banish the feeling of sadness gnawing at the corners of my mind.

Sura yawned. "Brother, I must thank ye again for saving me. 'Twas a noble thing of ye to do. Now if ye will excuse me, I must rest, for I am still in pain and need to give mine injuries time to heal."

"But are ye certain that ye are not going to join Reunification, brother?" I said. "If ye do, ye will be reunited with Kiriah again. No longer would our family be torn and apart; yea, we would be one once more."

Sura glanced at the three photographs again, then shook his head and said, "Whilst I do dearly wish to see our sister again, I would rather she come here and visit me than I go and see her. I have no interest in joining any secretive organization, for my duty lies with the Old Gods, as ye well know."

I sat back in mine chair, my shoulders slumping. This conversation 'twas not going the way I wanted it to at all. In mine head, I had expected Sura to agree to joining Reunification immediately so we could all be together again. That he refused, even if gently, was not something I had ever considered a serious possibility before.

Yet now I was faced with the idea that mine brother would always remain separate from us. The Founder had not wanted me to come here and speak with Sura, for he had said that he had important things for me to do on Xeeo. 'Twas thanks to Kiriah that I had been allowed to go at all, and even then, I had had to use one of Reunification's secret Portals to do so, in order to avoid drawing attention to my arrival on Dela.

"Ye seem disappointed, brother," said Sura, snapping me out of my thoughts. "I am sorry about that, but I hope ye understand my reasons. When ye return to this Reunification, ye can let Kiriah know that she is welcome to come back to the mansion any time she pleases."

I bit my lower lip, but nodded. "Yea, brother, I shall let her know that. I so wish ye could join us, but if ye do not want to, I will not force ye."

I stood up. "But please do not tell anyone about this organization. Reunification is supposed to be secret. 'Twas a great risk just coming here to tell ye about it. If word about this organization reaches the general public, it could ruin our plans, the plans we have been working toward for years."

Sura nodded. "Ye need not worry about that, brother. I have few visitors here, and of those few, I talk to them only briefly and about superficial matters. I hope that your organization is able to achieve its goals, even though I am not certain that they are achievable."

"Thank ye for the well wishes," I said. "I shall leave now. I must return to my allies, who are awaiting my return. The plan is so close to completion now that Kiriah says every hand is needed at the base, so I must leave with haste."

I turned to leave, but then I was interrupted by the distant sound of a motor, a sound that became less and less distant the longer I stood listening. Did sound like some vehicle was driving to the mansion, but I knew not who it could be, for the most advanced vehicle owned in Old Ways was the buggy, which had no engine or motor to make such a noise.

I looked over mine shoulder at Sura. "Brother, what is that sound I hear in mine ears? It sounds like a motor drawing ever closer to this mansion. Do ye hear it?"

"I do," said Sura. He gestured at the windows. "Why don't ye go and look out the windows to see if ye can spot it?"

I nodded and walked around Sura's bed toward the windows on the far side of the room. As carefully as I could, I pushed aside the thick curtains just enough for me to peek out the window and see what was out there.

As soon as I did, I almost jumped back. For driving up the road to the mansion's front gate was a four-wheeled vehicle with a clear domed cockpit, through which the morning sun's rays revealed two Knights of Se-Dela riding in it.

And I knew, beyond a shadow of a doubt, that the two Knights were coming for me.

Chapter Three

Quickly, I closed the curtains, turned, and made mine way to the door. Sura, who still lay in his bed, watched me go with surprise. He even sat up a little, saying, "Brother, where are ye—"

I stopped at the door and looked over mine shoulder at him. "Two of my fellow Knights are making their way up here even as we speak. Likely they are looking for me, which means I must flee before they can get here."

"But why?" said Sura. "I thought ye were a Knight yourself."

"Did your ears fail ye earlier, brother?" I said in annoyance. "I am no longer a Knight of Se-Dela. Nor do I have any interest in returning. I know what the punishment is for deserters and I have no intention of ever receiving that punishment. Good bye."

With that, I wrenched the door open and dashed out into the empty hallway. Here I could no longer hear the hum of the Diamusk vehicle's motor as it made its way toward this mansion, which made it nigh impossible for me to determine how close the Knights were to this place. Hence, I spent no time worrying; instead, I dashed toward the stairs, hoping to escape before the Knights arrived.

I climbed down the stairs with as much haste as I could, the sounds of my boots stomping against the wooden steps echoing off the walls of the stairwell. I could not believe mine rotten luck; Kiriah had assured me that there were no Knights of Se-Dela in the area today, yet I had seen with mine own eyes not one but two Knights. Yet I had no time to think about this strange turn of events; only to run, and to hopefully outrun their Diamusk.

Reaching the first floor—which was now much lighter, thanks to the rays of the rising morning sun peeking through the cracks in the shutters and curtains—I dashed down the hall in the direction of the back door of the mansion. Mine plan was to make it out through the back door, climb the fence surrounding the mansion, and run and hide in the wilderness until the Knights left. Then I would go and return to the Portal that would take me back to Reunification's Xeeonite headquarters, where I would be safe at last.

'Twas not long before I burst through the back door, nearly knocking it off its hinges, and emerged into the backyard of the mansion. I paid little attention to the tiny garden of vegetables to my right or the small pond to my left; instead, I made a mad dash for the fence, which was much taller than I.

I grasped the slim, cold, slightly damp bars of the fence and tried to lift mine self up. But I could find no traction, nor could I find a firm grip on the bars, or any footholds for me to place mine feet in. Mine hands slid down whenever I tried to pull myself up, though I still tried anyway.

Out here, I heard the sound of the Diamusk's motor drawing ever closer to the mansion; in fact, if mine ears were not deceiving me, then it sounded as though the motor was growing quieter and quieter, like the Knights were about to park it. That meant that I needed to climb out of here as fast as possible, for once the Knights arrived, I doubted I would be able to escape them.

Yet the fence was impossible to climb, and eventually I gave up. By the time I did, I heard the motor of the Diamusk shut off, followed by the sounds of the vehicle's doors opening and closing. They were on the other side of the mansion, but that meant little, for as the Knights of Se-Dela, they had full authority to check the premises of any property they wished. If they knocked on the front door and received no response—which was likely, seeing as Sura was still in bed and unable to walk much— then they might come 'round here, where they would discover me trying to escape.

I forced myself to calm down and think this through, for behaving irrationally 'twould not aid me much in this situation. Still, 'twas hard, for mine fear of the Knights did fill my soul and make me desire to run and hide.

I thought about running 'round the house, waiting until the two Knights entered, and then running out the gate, but with the sun already so high in the sky, I rejected it. Not only would the inhabitants of Old Ways see me, but so would the Knights, who would have no trouble catching up to me with their Diamusk vehicle.

Looking 'round the backyard, I searched for anything that could offer me a way out, perhaps something I could stand on to give me an extra bit of height I could use to climb out. But nay; 'twas nothing I could stand on, save some stones near the pond, although those stones were too small and round for me to stand on, even if I stacked them on top of each other.

Then I heard the voices of the two Knights—somewhat muffled and difficult to make out due to the mansion betwixt us— on the other side of the mansion. A sharp knock followed, and then one of the Knights yelled, "Lord Sura of the Moon Family! This is the Knights of Se-Dela. We have come in response to an anonymous tip stating that a man we are looking for is here. Open your door and let us in now."

I gulped. They were at the front door now, which meant it would not be long before they were inside. More likely, they would not come in through the front door, for Sura was still in bed. If they came 'round this way, then I would be well and truly caught.

It appeared, then, that I had only one option left: To go back into the mansion and hide in there until the Knights went away.

Yea, it did seem like a counterintuitive move, to be certain. For, after all, the Knights would likely search the mansion top and bottom for me, even if Sura were to tell them that I was not here. Yet I knew the mansion and its secrets far better than these two Knights. 'Twould not take much for me to find a good hiding place and wait until they left. Indeed, I was even now already thinking of such a place.

Thus, I turned and ran back into the house, but I opened the back door quietly, for I did not wish for the Knights to hear me enter. Stepping back into the mudroom, I closed the door behind me just as I heard the front door slam open, which no doubt meant that the Knights had decided to use their authority to enter without mine brother's permission.

But I did not allow my fear to overwhelm me. Relying on mine memory, I made my way through the darkened hallway even as I listened to the sounds of the Knight's heavy footfalls and the clinking of their armor enter the mansion. The room I was thinking of hiding in was on the second floor, but there was clearly no way I could climb up to the second floor when the Knights were now in the house.

Instead, I felt along the smooth wooden walls of the hall, searching for that secret closet I knew to be here. Our family mansion had many hiding places and secret entrances; indeed, I did not even know all of them, though I knew most.

As I felt along the walls, I heard the footfalls and armor clinking of the Knights drawing ever closer. Whilst the Knights did not need to pass through this hall in order to reach the stairs leading to the second floor, I was still a sitting duck out here, and they would likely notice me on their way to the upper floors, if they did not simply decide to do a thorough sweep of the first floor first before moving on.

Thus, I searched frantically for that panel that I knew would open up the secret closet. This did feel like déjà vu, although I was not certain why. Perhaps it 'twas because I had hidden in this closet when I was younger, although it seemed like I was trying to remember something else, for the back of mine head did ache when I tried to remember.

Then I felt the irregular wood panel and pushed it in. Once I did so, the closet door popped open to mine left. With the sounds of the Knights' footfalls drawing ever closer, I pulled open the door, dashed inside, and closed it shut, though I did it quietly to avoid drawing their attention to my location.

Locking the door, I stepped back and sighed in relief. 'Twas a close one, that had been, for I had been certain that I was going to be captured and arrested. I knew that the Knights could not find me here, so all I needed to do was sit back and be as quiet as possible until the Knights left. Then I could leave and return to Xeeo, where I could resume aiding my allies in completing the Mission.

Unfortunately for me, the closet was quite narrow and short, much narrower and shorter than I remembered it being. The top of mine head almost scraped across the ceiling, my elbows knocked into the shelves on either side, and it was suffocatingly hot in here. Not to mention I discovered thick layers of dust on the shelves and walls, which told me that it had been years since someone had last been in here. 'Twas no surprise to me, however, because I had never told anyone, even the other members of my family, about this closet.

Perhaps the worst thing about this place was the lack of a chair or a stool or even an upturned bucket to sit on. This struck me as exceedingly odd, for I thought I remembered finding something to sit on in here when I was younger. Perhaps I sat on the floor, although considering how small this closet was, even that seemed doubtful.

The closet, also, smelled dry and musky, which made breathing difficult, for there was dust in the air that tried to enter mine lungs. I wanted to cough, but I held mine breath, for if I coughed, that would certainly give away my position to the searching Knights.

But I did not complain. Instead, I closed mine eyes and prayed to the Old Gods to protect me and Sura from these Knights. It did not seem likely that they would harm Sura—for despite not being adherents of the Old Gods, many of the Knights still respected priests like mine brother. Still, I asked for the Old Gods' protection anyway, just to be safe.

Then I listened. I heard the two Knights stomping throughout the first floor, opening drawers, throwing open closet doors, and searching through everything. It did not sound like the Knights were breaking or damaging the furniture; still, I burned with anger at the thought of them going through the heirlooms of my family, which no one was allowed to touch save for mine siblings and I.

A moment later, I heard the two sets of footfalls coming around the hall. 'Twas hard to distinguish betwixt the two, for the two Knights sounded close in size and weight. Nevertheless, I was able to discern that at least one of them was slightly heavier than the other based on the weight of their steps, although I knew nothing else about them.

"What'd you find?" said one of the Knights, his voice quite familiar to me, though at first I was not sure where I had heard it before. "Any sign of him?"

"No," said a feminine voice, which I immediately pegged as Lady Euha's, a she-elf and former Knight friend of mine. "Nothing. I don't see any sign of Apakerec anywhere."

"We haven't checked the next two floors yet," said the male voice, which I now recognized as belonging to Sir Alart, another former comrade of mine. "For that matter, where's his brother? I thought he lived here."

"He's probably in the upper floors," said Lady Euha. "Although I am starting to think that this whole thing is a waste of time. No one has seen hide nor hair of Apakerec for two and a half weeks, and suddenly he's supposed to be here?"

"Hey, it was Sir Lockfried who got the anonymous tip," said Sir Alart. "And when Sir Lockfried orders us to do something, we do it, even if it doesn't make sense."

"Yeah, I know," said Lady Euha. "Still, I have a good feeling that we're not going to find anything."

"Believe that if you want, but for now, we have a deserter to find," said Sir Alart. "Let's go to the upper floors. He might be hiding up there."

Mine nose twitched, but I did not give mine self the luxury of sneezing, even though I desperately wanted to. At least, I tried to hold it in, even with the dust floating around in the air. Mine eyes watered badly to the point where it was like trying to look through the windshield of a Diamusk driving through a torrential rain.

I just needed to hold it in a little while longer … just a little while longer … and I would be—

Without warning, mine nose exploded not once, not twice, but three times. Every sneeze 'twas like a cannon being fired, a sound amplified in the tiny closet I stood in. And with every explosive sneeze, more dust was unsettled, which went into mine lungs and made me cough like a mad man.

"What is that?" Sir Alart said above the sounds of my sneezes. "Where is that sneezing and coughing sound coming from?"

"Sounds like it's coming from this wall," said Lady Euha. "Now I know that Apakerec's family's mansion is supposed to be strange, but I think that sneezing walls takes the cake for weird magical—"

Without hesitation, I unlocked and then burst through the closet door. The door slammed into Lady Euha, who fell to the floor, her metalligick armor clanking against the wood underneath her.

Turning to run down the hall, I found myself standing before Sir Alart. He was looking at me in pure shock; at least, his left, organic eye was, while his mechanical eye zoomed in and out like he had lost control of it.

"Rii?" said Sir Alart, who had not even drawn his sword. "What the—"

I drew my skyras sword and activated it. The energy blade extended with a loud hiss, which I swung at my former partner's head.

Sir Alart ducked, but then I kicked him in the face. The blow sent him staggering backwards, but I did not let him recover. I dashed forward and knocked him to the floor with my shoulder, where he fell with a *clang*, and then I dashed down the hall toward the living room. Even so, I could already hear both Alart and Euha rising again, which meant it would not be long before they came after me once more.

Hence, when I entered the living room, I leaped over the sofa, landed hard on the floor on both feet, and then dashed toward the mudroom. Just as I was about to exit the living room, Sir Alart appeared in the doorway, causing me to skid to a halt (and wonder for a moment how he had managed to intercept me so quickly). I stepped backwards as Sir Alart drew his sword and advanced on me.

"Now, now, Rii, don't you try to run from us," said Sir Alart, who pointed his sword at mine chest, keeping me from leaving the living room, whilst holding his shield close to his own chest. "We're not your enemies. We just want you to come with us so you can tell Sir Lockfried where you have been for the last two and a half weeks."

I heard footsteps behind me and glanced over mine shoulder. Euha stood in the entrance to the living room that I had come through. Like Alart, she carried her sword at an offensive angle and her shield defensively. Whilst I could perhaps handle one Knight on mine own, fighting two at once made me doubt mine own abilities.

"Put down your weapon," said Sir Alart, without putting down his own. "We're not interested in hurting you. We just want to talk."

I kept mine mouth shut, not because I had nothing to say to Alart or Euha, but because I did not want to tell either of them about Reunification. They were not even supposed to know I was here; why then should I speak to them at all? Nay, 'twas better to fight than to stand here and reveal all of Reunification's secrets to those who might stand against us.

Hence, I stepped back a few more steps, still holding my skyras sword before me, trying to think of some way to get past Alart. And I had to think quickly, for Euha was already advancing toward me from the other side of the room, her metalligick armor clanking with every step. 'Twould not be long before they apprehended me.

Yet I could not run; therefore, I would fight.

I charged at Alart, swinging mine skyras sword at him. He seemed taken aback by this sudden attack of mine, for he only just managed to raise his shield in time to block my blow. Mine energy blade hissed against the metal of his shield, but then his shield glowed blue and it ceased melting under the heat of my blade, likely due to the skyras energy flowing from the metalligick armor into the shield itself.

I pushed hard against his shield nonetheless, forcing Sir Alart backwards, although not by much, for his armor added an extra weight to him that made him harder to push away. He then swung his blade at me, forcing me to jump back to avoid being cut into.

When I landed on my feet again, I heard another blade whistling through the air behind me and I ducked. Euha's sword flew over my head, almost scraping mine scalp. I then whirled around and slashed at her, but she blocked the blow with her own shield, which, like Alart's, glowed with the skyras energy protecting it from mine blade.

Then I heard Alart running over to us, forcing me to whirl around again and slash at him. He held up his shield again, blocking mine blade easily, though this time I did not try to push him back, for I heard Euha swinging her sword at me again.

So I ducked and rolled forward across the hard wood floor, again avoiding Euha's sword, and then rolled back to mine feet. Holding up mine blade before me, I stepped back as Alart and Euha turned to advance toward me, forcing me to walk backwards toward the glass case containing the ancient silverware passed down through mine family for generations.

"This is your last chance, Rii," said Alart, his tone full of warning, slightly muffled through his helmet's visor. "If you put your weapon down and give up, then we can take you in without hurting you. Okay?"

"Nay," I said, with as much emphasis on that word as I could so as to leave no doubt that I did not wish to surrender so easily.

"All right," said Alart. "But don't say I didn't warn you."

I almost backed into the glass case containing mine family's silverware, which forced me to stop and stay where I was. This time, I truly had no way to escape, for both Alart and Euha had blocked off mine escape routes and there was no exit behind me I could use.

Just as the two Knights and their swords came within reach of me, I saw movement from the shadowy corners of the living room. Thought 'twas nothing more than a trick of the eye before two shadow hands burst from the corners and grabbed Alart and Euha as easily as a large fish in a small pond.

Alart let out a yell of fear, while Euha gasped. The two swung their swords at the shadow hands, but the hands did not let go. If anything, their resistance seemed to embolden the hands, for their grip tightened around the Knights' waists.

Then the hands lifted up the two Knights and threw them at the ceiling. They were thrown so quickly that I barely understood what I was seeing, but then I saw them fall to the floor and lay there, still and unmoving. They had dropped their weapons, but the tubing that sent skyras energy into their equipment was still connected to their armor. Still, 'twas very clear to me now that these two were unlikely to wake any time soon.

The shadow hands immediately retreated into the corners from which they came. At the same time, I heard Sura yell, "Rii! Are ye all right?"

I looked toward the living room entrance in which Alart had been standing earlier and saw Sura leaning against the archway. He looked like he must have struggled to get down here, for he was panting and looked exceedingly tired. His face 'twas still bandaged and he had a blanket 'round his shoulders as if to keep him warm, though his hands looked sweaty even from where I stood.

"Sura?" I said in alarm. "Brother, what are ye doing out of bed? I thought ye were too tired to get up."

Panting, Sura said, "Yea, brother, I was indeed weak and tired, but when I heard the sound of battle 'neath mine bed, I had to aid ye. After all, ye are mine brother and I was not about to let mine brother be punished by his former allies, not when I could do something about it."

Sura struggled to say each word; that surprised me not, for mine brother looked close to fainting now. I would not be shocked if he were to immediately fall down right now, which is why I ran over to him and put an arm 'round his shoulder to support him.

"Thank ye, brother, for your aid," I said. Then I looked at Alart and Euha, who still lay unconscious on the floor. "But if these two awake and discover that ye aided me in mine escape, then they will undoubtedly arrest ye for helping a deserter. 'Tis a crime punishable by life imprisonment."

Sura nodded. "Ye, I was aware of that. And I am ready to handle the consequences for any decision of mine that helps mine family, regardless of its legality."

"Nay," I said, shaking my head. "Ye must come with me to Reunification, where we will be safe from all law enforcement. I cannot stand the thought of mine older brother being arrested and interrogated by mine former allies in an attempt to find out where I have gone, especially after all ye have gone through today."

"Thank ye for the offer, brother," said Sura, putting one hand on my shoulder. He looked me in the eyes while speaking. "But I ... but I ..."

Sura was clearly losing his consciousness. His good eye kept blinking open and close and he began to feel heavier under mine arm, forcing me to put more effort into keeping him upright. All of the pain and excitement of the day was catching up with him; indeed, I was shocked that he had managed to make it this far without collapsing.

Then his head went limp on his shoulder and his eye closed. At the same time, he nearly fell, but I redoubled my grip and kept him upright, though 'twas a challenge, for he was heavier than he appeared.

"Rest ye well, brother," I said as I shut off mine skyras sword and placed it back in its sheath under mine robes. "For I shall take ye to safety, where none of our enemies will find us."

Chapter Four

I had to carry mine brother with both of my arms, though due to my strength, that 'twas not as difficult as it might have been. Whilst Sura was hardly as light as our sister, carrying him was closer to carrying around several sacks of potatoes than a flower.

Before I carried him, however, I rested him on the floor in a comfortable position and then searched Alart and Euha's bodies for the keys to their Diamusk. For I intended to take the Diamusk and use it to return to the Portal I had used to get here; with the sun now high in the sky, 'twas no way I could carry mine brother out through Old Ways without being spotted by every man, woman, and child in that village.

I did found the keys on Sir Alart, along with a dozen other keys I could not identify. As I did not need these others, I slipped the Diamusk key off the ring and slipped it into the pockets of my robes.

After that, I returned and picked up Sura, who had not so much as uttered one word since losing consciousness. 'Twas not a problem for me, for the quieter he kept, the easier it was for me to concentrate.

We went out through the front door, which was still open due to the Knights forgetting to shut it earlier. As soon as I stepped out, I spotted the Diamusk just outside the front gate: A four-wheeled vehicle with a dome-like cockpit. It was painted silver and blue, the official colors of Diamusk vehicles driven by the Knights of Se-Dela, and it had two seats; one for the driver, the other for the passenger. I paid little attention to it, however, because I had seen and driven many Diamusk vehicles during mine time as a Knight of Se-Dela and this one looked no more different from or special than any other.

When I stepped out onto the front porch of our mansion, however, I did not walk toward the Diamusk. Instead, I turned and looked up at our home, for I realized that this 'twas likely the last time I would see it for a long time, perhaps forever. Or at least until the Mission was complete and Dela and Xeeo were one once more, though for all I knew our home might not survive the reunification process.

That thought made mine heart sink, for despite some of the negative memories I did associate with that house, it was still mine childhood home. Not only that, but it had been built on the foundations of an ancient temple of the Old Gods that had been destroyed eons ago, which made it even more important to me.

Nonetheless, I knew I had to leave the mansion behind. Nor could I take anything with us, for I had little time to search for family heirlooms and keepsakes. Nay, I did not even go back for the Divine Books; whilst that thought of leaving behind those books did indeed make me feel shameful, I knew that they were not terribly important in the long run. After all, once the Mission was complete, then it would not matter whether or not the Divine Books were with us, for then we could work to free the Old Gods from their prison on the moon. 'Twas mine thought on the matter, anyway.

Besides, there was the practical matter of bringing the Divine Books with us. Most Diamusk vehicles had little room for tomes as thick as those. Certain types of Diamusks were large enough to carry equipment and other things, but this particular type that Alart and Euha had driven here was hardly big enough for two people. 'Twas better to save my brother and I than try to get the books as well. But perhaps someday I would return to get them, though I doubted it.

Thus, with one final look at mine childhood home, I turned and walked toward the gates, though not without feeling a last pang of regret for abandoning our home as well.

After sitting Sura upright and buckling him in, I sat in the driver's seat. The air of the Diamusk was much colder than the outside, though that did not shock me much, for the Diamusk could generate cold air thanks to some mysterious Xeeonite technology I did not understand. I understood also that Euha had likely demanded that the interior temperature be this cold, for the she-elf had always been more warm-blooded than most of us and thus was not as tolerant of warmer temperatures as most Knights were.

I also recalled why I never liked these vehicles in the first place. Whilst Diamusks were indeed much faster and could carry more people than horses (which were the original steeds of the Knights of Se-Dela prior to being replaced by these machines some years ago), they were still quite cramped, especially these smaller models, which I was convinced were constructed by Xeeonites who wanted to make us curse the heavens.

Still, it was not as cramped as it could have been, perhaps, because I was not wearing mine old metalligick armor. And at least I recalled how to active and operate it, which I did by inserting the key into the ignition and turning it.

The Diamusk engine roared to life, a noise so loud that I could barely hear myself think. Sura stirred and muttered something under his breath, but he did not awake. 'Twas good, because I did not want him to awake just yet.

Thus, I backed up the Diamusk as quickly as I could and then we were rumbling down the road from our mansion as fast as I could go. In the Diamusk's rearview mirrors, I caught a glimpse of our old home, which still stood proud and tall on that hill, though I took mine eyes off the mirror to focus on the road ahead.

The tiny village of Old Ways was now alive. As I drove closer to the town, I saw old men sitting on chairs on their front porches, elderly wives working in the gardens in front of their houses, and the younger men and women performing some of the more physically intense work, such as carrying heavy bags of vegetables or knocking fence posts into the earth. Seeing these people brought more memories to mind, such as the many times when my brother and I would aid our elderly neighbors during our childhood.

But I gave myself no time to dwell on those memories, nor did I stop to say hello to any of my old friends and neighbors (oddly enough, however, I could barely recall the names or faces of most of them). I simply drove the Diamusk straight through the village, scaring some chickens that had been crossing the road and causing more than a few curious heads to turn and watch us speed by.

Soon, the village of Old Ways was behind us. I wondered for

a moment if any of the villagers had recognized either of us through the windshield, although I doubted it, for I had not driven slowly enough for them to make out who had been driving this vehicle. Still, they would all know soon enough, once Sir Alart and Lady Euha awoke and summoned reinforcements from Ra-Dela, the capital city of the country.

Beyond Old Ways was little more than a long, winding gravel road and in the distance I could see the Cyclone Mountains and beyond them was the city of Ra-Dela, even though I could not see it right now. There were scattered towns and villages betwixt here and the Cyclone Mountains, but I had no intention of visiting any of them.

Instead, once I passed 'round a hill that was well away from the village, I parked the Diamusk vehicle behind it and stepped out. The sun was higher in the sky now; not high enough to be too hot, but 'twas noticeably warmer now than it was before. Of course, the interior temperature of the Diamusk was much colder than the outside, which perhaps explained why it felt warmer to me.

In any case, I unbuckled and lifted Sura out of the Diamusk. While I would have loved to take the vehicle with me, I did not want the Knights to track down this Diamusk to the secret Portal I had used to get here in the first place. For if I did that, then Reunification would indeed be compromised, and the Mission might not be completed at all. A terrifying and depressing thought, to be sure.

Hence, I would make mine way to the Portal on foot the rest of the way. 'Twould not be terribly difficult, for I knew where the Portal was, although I would have to hurry, for the heat of the day would undoubtedly become worse as the day aged, and Sura was not exactly a light figure to carry around, either.

After making certain that I had not forgotten anything in the Diamusk ('twas unlikely, of course, for I had not brought much with me in the first place), I made my way through the tall grass as quickly as I could with Sura in my arms. This time, I looked not back at the vehicle I had left behind, for I now did not care much for it outside of its usefulness in getting me and mine brother away from our old home.

'Twas only a few minutes later that I found what I was looking for: A solid rock wall that led seemingly nowhere. And indeed, for those who knew not what it was, this wall did indeed lead nowhere; however, I knew exactly what it was and so I understood that it was mine ticket out of this place.

Without hesitation, I walked through the rock wall, which was no rock wall at all, but rather an illusion. 'Twas created by one of Reunification's cameras, which hung off the ceiling in the cave I had entered, constantly projecting the image of that rock wall to the outside. I did not understand exactly how it worked, but I did not need to, for it worked whether I understood it or not.

The cave I had entered was a tall one and appeared to have been dug out at some point, but by who or why, I knew not. All I knew was that the cave, due to its obscure location, was the perfect hiding place for a secret Portal connecting Dela to Xeeo, especially a Portal for Reunification. The air in here was cooler than outside, though not as cold as the interior of the Diamusk had been.

And indeed, I did see the Portal I had used earlier this morning, when the sun 'twas still awaking. This Portal, like most

Delanian Portals, appeared to be made out of stone and rock; unlike other Portals, however, this one was much smaller, slightly taller than mine self, in order to fit inside this cave. It had been placed here by Reunification operatives in order to give us another way of getting to Dela without the governments of either world knowing.

I stepped up to the Portal, which was currently inactive, and said, "Portal, activate."

When I said that, there was silence for a few seconds. Then the Portal's ring began to glow red, and a second later, a swirling vortex of bluish white and a watery texture appeared within it. I could not see what was on the other side, but I did not need to, for I knew exactly what lay beyond the vortex.

After making certain that I held Sura securely in mine arms, I stepped through the Portal without hesitation.

Although I had traveled through Crossways Portals many times in the past, it was still a disorienting experience. The period when I was between Dela and Xeeo was confusing and terrifying, for wherever I looked, I saw nothing but more of the strange colors and textures of the vortex. Mine ears were bombarded with the crackling of electricity in the air around me, and for a moment I could barely breathe.

Thankfully, I was in that limbo for only a moment. The next instant, I was on the other side, shivering and shaking slightly from the Portal's effect on mine body, but otherwise whole and well. Sura was still in mine arms, although he had ceased stirring, which was good, because he needed to be still in order to heal.

Yet mine eyes did take a moment to adjust to the change in lighting. 'Twas one of the few aftereffects of Portal travel that I still struggled with, for I still saw the vortex's frightening and confusing appearance even after stepping out of he Portal. I had been told once, long ago, by a Delanian wizard that that was known as the 'Portal sight effect,' which afflicted only a small group of people on both worlds, but whatever it was, it did make me feeling exceedingly uncomfortable and sick.

Still, it lasted only a few seconds, by which time mine vision had cleared up and I could see my environment.

I had stepped into the part of Reunification's headquarters known as the Portal Chamber. 'Twas a large, underground stone chamber above the dungeons but 'neath the upper floors, with dozens of Portals that led to places all over Dela and Xeeo. Around me stood those Portals; some were the same size as mine, while others were much taller and wider. One such Portal was so tall that it touched the ceiling; an impressive feat, for the ceiling of this Chamber was fifteen feet in height.

But I focused not on the Chamber. Instead, I made mine way down the steps to the floor, for I needed to get Sura to the medical room immediately. Whilst he was by no means in danger of dying, at least from what I could see, he still required medical attention in order to more fully treat his wounds. Besides, I did worry that he might be hurt worse than either of us knew and therefore needed the expertise of our doctors to make certain that he was fine.

As I walked betwixt the Portals, however, I saw two beings walking toward me hurriedly. One was a Jikorian, those humanoid Xeeonite creatures with large foreheads and a painted-on-looking light green skin, though he wore a cloak much like mine, rather than the typical leather jackets I usually associated with the Jikorians. The other was a human, short and ugly, looking so dwarf-like that I at times almost mistook him for one (although this particular human had corrected me—and by no means politely—several times that he 'twas no dwarf and that he had no dwarfish blood flowing through his veins).

I almost groaned when I saw them, but I refrained from doing so, for they were members of Reunification just as I was. Still, I was no fan of these two, for they were not very smart, to put it lightly, nor did I get 'long with them well. Every time I saw them, I wanted to go the other way, even though they were members of Reunification same as I.

"Arn and Lauz," I said, stopping as I watched them approach. "What brings ye down here to the Chamber? Are ye going somewhere?"

"Yes," said Lauz, the Jikorian, nodding as the two of them stopped together not far from me. "Got to go to Xeeon for a top secret mission given to us by ya sister."

Arn, the tiny human, kicked Lauz in the shin and said, "You idiot. You call his sister the *Leader*. Don't act like we're her best friends or anything like that."

Lauz rubbed his shin and said, "Uh, ya right, Arn. Almost forgot."

"You better not," said Arn, shaking a fist at him. "Or else I'll do much worse to you than just kick your shin. Got it?"

Their antics did not amuse me, so I said, "Fellow agents, please move out of mine way, for in my arms lies mine brother, who desperately needs medical attention. I must also report back to Kiriah on the status of my mission."

"Oh, yeah," said Arn, snapping his fingers. "Almost forgot.

Kir—I mean, the Leader did say that she wanted us to go and check on your status before we left for Xeeon, because no one has heard from you in a while. Had something important she wanted us to tell you, right, Lauz?"

"Right," said Lauz, nodding and smiling, apparently forgetting all about Arn kicking his shin not more than ten seconds ago. "Yeah, I remember. But, uh, what was it?"

Arn sighed. "We were supposed to tell Rii to go and meet with the Leader in the pit. Don't tell me you forgot that already."

"I guess I did," said Lauz. He stepped away from Arn. "Please don't kick my shin. Twice in one day is enough for me."

"What does mine sister wish to speak with me about?" I asked. "And why meet in the pit, of all places? Did she say why she wished to converse with me?"

"She didn't say," said Arn, shaking his head and folding his arms over his chest. "She just told us to tell you to go and see her as soon as you got back."

I frowned. Whilst I enjoyed speaking with mine sister, I knew that she would not summon me to speak with her privately unless it was something of great importance. As the Leader of Reunification, she had little time to set aside to talk with me as much as I liked, which always bothered me, for it had been six years since her disappearance and yet I still could not speak with her regularly save for meetings or during mission briefings.

That was why I took every opportunity I could to speak with mine sister, so I said, "All right. I will go and meet her in the pit as soon as I take Sura to the medical room."

"Hey, why don't you let us take your brother to the medical room?" said Arn. "We can carry him between us. That way, you can go and meet the Leader without wasting time."

"Forgive me, Arn, but I am not quite so interested in letting ye two carry mine brother," I said, holding Sura closer to my chest. "He has had a rough day and needs to be handled gently, more gently than either of ye two are capable of, I regret to say."

"We can be gentle," said Arn, jabbing a thumb at his chest. "Right, Lauz?"

"Uh, right," said Lauz, nodding, although I could tell that he had not been listening to our conversation, which did little to build up my trust in him. "Gentle as a kite."

I bit my lower lip. I really did not trust either of them with even the simplest of tasks (which often made me wonder why mine sister even employed them, for they were nothing more than a couple of bumbling fools who made portal monkeys look like intelligent scholars).

But I also knew that Kiriah could be quite impatient. She loathed waiting for anything, which I believe to be a result of her being the youngest and therefore most spoiled of us three siblings (though I of course kept such thoughts to mine self, for I also knew Kiriah did not appreciate being called spoiled even if it was true).

Seeing as I did not wish to anger mine sister, I sighed and said, "All right. Take Sura to the medical machines immediately. Do not delay or attempt to take any shortcuts. And if either ye harm him at all, then ye will have to answer to me. Understood?"

Both Arn and Lauz nodded as solemnly as Sura whenever he performed one of the rites of the Old Gods. I was hardly reassured by that, but seeing as I had already agreed to let them take Sura, I gave mine brother over to them and watched as they carried him away toward the elevator on the other side of the Chamber.

I supposed Sura would be all right, because neither Arn nor Lauz was dumb enough to anger me. Already, they had seen mine sharp temper, for once the two had nearly closed a Portal on my hand, which would have resulted in me losing that hand. Thankfully, I did not lose it, but I still remembered quite vividly how terrified I had been when I thought that I was going to have one less hand than I 'twas born with.

Shaking mine head, I turned down the left, walking between Portal after Portal lined up on either side of the path. I was heading toward the other elevator, the one that would take me outside to the site of the pit. I could have taken the elevator with Arn and Lauz as well, but this one would take me directly there; besides, I loathed the idea of being stuck in an elevator with those two buffoons for even five minutes.

Upon approaching the elevator, I hesitated. Though I had used this particular elevator several times over the last two and a half weeks, still I trusted not this odd contraption found in many Xeeonite buildings that were taller than two stories. Elevators were small and cramped, and mine heart always seemed to drop to mine stomach when I was going up or get caught in my throat when I was going down.

Still, I would have taken the stairs if they were closer or faster, but seeing as the Portal Chamber had no stairs leading down to it at all, I was forced to use this elevator. I had considered speaking with Kiriah several times about adding in stairs to this headquarters, but I always decided against it, for we were now so close to completing the Mission that it made no sense to divert important resources and manpower to building a

81

staircase leading underground, resources and manpower that could instead be used to dig the pit even deeper than before.

With some hesitation, I pressed the up arrow on the elevator's control pad to the right of its doors. A moment later, a small *ding* told me that the elevator had arrived. The twin doors opened slowly and automatically, which made me step back involuntarily, for despite having spent much time on Xeeo, the idea of doors sliding open on their own 'twas still one I had difficulty adapting to even under the best of circumstances.

But I pushed past my initial hesitation and stepped into the elevator, which did shudder slightly under mine feet. I almost worried that the cable holding the elevator would snap and send me crashing down the shaft inside this machine, but the elevator car held and the doors closed behind me without a noise. A speaker hung in one corner, from which important proclamations from Kiriah would come every now and then, though today the speaker 'twas silent.

I was not quite as used to the elevator as a Xeeonite native; however, upon joining Reunification, Kiriah had shown me how it worked. I knew that the topmost button would lead me to where I needed to go, so I reached for it with mine index finger.

Just as I was about to press the topmost button, the speaker behind me crackled like lightning. The sudden crackling sound did make me jump, causing the elevator to bounce up and down briefly, once again making me fear that I would meet my bloody end at the bottom of the elevator's shaft.

As always, however, the elevator held, but the speaker continued to crackle and it did make me stare at it uncertainly. Was there some sort of interference on Kiriah's end causing her announcement to fail to come out? Or was this speaker somehow damaged? If it 'twas, there was nothing I could do about it, for I knew little about repairing machines such as this. Perhaps I could inform one of our resident technicians to take a look at it later and —

"Help!" a voice—weak and crackly through the speaker— shouted. "Anyone there? Please help me … this place is horrible … can barely speak … oh, my legs …"

I stared at the speaker in amazement and fear. I backed up to the corner furthest from the speaker, but 'twas a pointless gesture, for there was nowhere in here for me to run to or hide inside. Yet despite my fear, I thought I recognized the voice, although I could not place where or when I had heard it before.

"Please," said the voice, which sounded so terrified and pleading that I also began to feel sorry for it. "Help, help, whoever you are. I can't escape on my own. Apakerec, if you're out there, do you hear me?"

Mine eyes widened. How did this voice know mine name? Did make no sense, for I knew not the name of whoever 'twas on the opposite end of that speaker. For that matter, how was this person, whoever he was, able to speak through that machine? I had thought that only Kiriah had access to the microphone which fed into the speaker. Was this a fellow member of Reunification or someone else?

"Please, help me," said the voice again. "Apakerec, if you hear me, come to the dungeons. You might not recognize my voice, so I'll tell you my name. It's Re—"

The speaker cut off abruptly there, before I could hear the rest of his name. Mine heart beating, I did not move from the corner of the elevator where I had backed into, for I was still processing all that I had heard.

According to that voice, there was someone in the dungeons below the Portal Chamber. I found that odd. For whilst I had known about the dungeons for sometime, I had not known that there was anyone in it. Kiriah had assured me that the dungeons were usually kept empty and only there in case a rogue Reunification member needed to be kept somewhere out of the way for a little while.

Yet this person did not sound to me like any Reunification member I knew of. Granted, I did not know every one of my fellow Reunification members, for there were many scattered across both Dela and Xeeo. For example, I had never met Kalcan, an arctic vampire and one of the three Elders in charge of the Delanian operations, though I had heard many rumors of his terrible might and power.

Still, I did not think that a member of Reunification would hack into Kiriah's speaker and use it to send a message of distress out to the rest of the organization. Did make no sense. Nay, only a non-member would even think of doing that, for anyone else who tried to use Kiriah's microphone would be punished severely for this crime.

I peeled mine self off the corner and stood still, listening for the speaker. It did not activate again, though I was hoping for an explanation from someone. That there was no answer did make me wonder if I was the only one to hear it or if my fellow Reunification agents had heard it also; and if so, what they were intending to do about it.

But more importantly, I had to find out who that was. This

man, whoever he was, knew mine name and called for me specifically. Why, when I did not even know what his face looked like, I could not say; hence, why I had to find out.

Yet I also had to go and meet Kiriah. I loathed missing our meetings or rejecting her orders to come and speak with her, but this mystery was too tempting for me to simply ignore. Besides, I doubted it would take me very long to head down to the dungeons and see who was down there and crying for help. 'Twould not hurt me; after all, it sounded like the prisoner was unable to so much as walk, so I doubt he could do much to me even if he had nothing but ill intentions for me.

Thus, I came to mine decision: I would go down to the dungeons and see who was down there. I would only be down there for a brief time, perhaps a few minutes at most; after that, I would head back up and go meet with Kiriah again.

Besides, I thought, as I pressed the lowest button on the console and the elevator began going down, if this prisoner had indeed hacked unjustly into Kiriah's microphone, then that would be mine job to teach him what happens to those who use my sister's audio equipment without her permission.

'Twas only a couple of minutes later that the elevator reached the dungeons and opened. Stepping out of the elevator, I looked around at the dark, dank dungeons, wrinkling mine nose at its stale smell. I so rarely came down here that I did not really know what to expect; indeed, the last time I remembered coming down here was two and a half weeks ago, when Kiriah gave me a tour of the building. Nay; not even then. As a matter of fact, I could not ever remember coming down here. Perhaps the feeling of déjà vu I felt upon coming here was false.

In any case, the dungeons were dark and had none of those electric lights that the rest of the building had. I groped mine hand along the dusty stone wall to mine right, but could not find the light switch. That did seem odd to me; whilst I understood that the dungeons were, by definition, not supposed to be good places to be, it did seem strange that they apparently lacked any sort of power at all.

The only light 'twas the light of the elevator, which spilled out of the open doorway. Even then, that light revealed little, except for the metal bars of empty jail cells, bars which were as black and rusted as the old suits of armor I once saw in the storage basement of Castle Una when I first joined the Knights of Se-Dela.

But I was not afraid, for as an agent of Reunification, I could not allow fear to constrain me. For if fear defined mine life, then I would be unable to aid in completing the Mission, a thought that made me shudder.

Still, I prayed a quick prayer to the Old Gods, for I still relied on them for guidance and protection. Whether they could hear me in this place, I knew not, for the Old Gods presided over Dela and not Xeeo. 'Twas a habit, praying to them was, although one I had done far less of ever since joining Reunification.

With that prayer out of the way, I walked out of the elevator— which closed behind me—into the darkness, turning my head this way and that as I walked past the cells. Most were empty; indeed, they looked as if they had not been used for years, perhaps even decades. From one cell gave the smell of moldy bread and what might have been dried blood; from another, I heard something small scurrying through the shadows, perhaps a mouse of some sort, although as far as I knew there were no mice in Reunification's headquarters.

Through it all, I heard not one sound of any prisoner. Indeed, the further I walked, the more I began to believe that perhaps there really were not any prisoners down here, like I had been fooled into believing that man's voice over the speaker. Perhaps it had been some sort of bizarre prank, but then I remembered how desperate and fearful that voice had sounded, and I found it hard to believe that it was the voice of some sort of prankster. Especially considering the punishment for those who used Kiriah's microphone, which I didst not think was worth whatever enjoyment a prankster could get from such a joke.

Then, through the darkness, I heard the sound of claws scraping against the stone floor. I stopped and listened, but I didst not hear the sound again, which made me wonder if I had been hearing things. Did seem unlikely to me, however, for mine hearing was excellent and I rarely heard things that were not there; even so, in this dark place, I felt more than a little hesitant about charging headfirst into the shadows when I knew not the source of that sound.

Steeling myself for whatever was down there, I continued walking, but slowly now, keeping mine ears wide open, paying more careful attention to the sounds of this place than I did before. I considered yelling to find out who was here, but I felt it would be safer to keep silent for now.

To aid me in seeing where I was, I drew mine skyras sword from mine sheath and pressed the tab. The skyras blade immediately appeared; whilst it was much brighter than the darkness, mine sword had not been designed to act as a torch, and consequently I could not see much more than I already could before.

As soon as the blade of mine sword extended, I heard more clicking and clacking of talons against the stone floor. It did not sound like it was getting closer to me, but 'twas so sudden that I took a defensive stance anyway.

"Hello?" said a voice from within the darkness, the same voice as the one on the speaker, although it sounded more natural now, without the static of the speaker to distort it. "Who's there? Apakerec, is that you?"

I was surprised to hear the hope in his voice. 'Twas like he thought I was going to be his savior, although I understood not why he would think that, for I did not even know his name. Thus, I was on high alert now, for this all struck me as very suspicious.

Still, I said, "Yea, it is I. Who spake to me?"

"R-Resita," said the voice, which sounded only a few cells down from mine current position. "Don't you remember me at all?"

I walked down the line of cells on the right side, looking at each one until the light of mine skyras sword showed me a sight I would never forget.

In one of the smaller and narrower cells lay a Checrom, a member of a species of bird-like humanoids that lived primarily in Xeeo. We had a couple of Checrom agents in Reunification, though I rarely spent time with them, for often they were in other parts of the world performing tasks and missions that I knew little of.

But this Checrom lying in the cell before me lacked the

beautiful plumage or sharpened talons of the Checrom I knew. His feathers might have at one point been a brilliant yellow, but in the green light of mine energy blade, they looked a sickening yellow-green. And most of his feathers were missing or lying on the floor all around him, making him look as pitiful as a newborn chick.

And his talons were blunted and even cracked in places. He was huddled up against the back wall, wiring from the speaker above his head in his grasp. His eyes were an odd color, somewhere betwixt green and brown, but it was not the color that caught me, but his look of fear and hope. The wiring he held was attached to an empty metal bowl, though I understood not how he had made it work.

His legs, in particular, looked terribly thin. I would have thought them broken, had I not seen them move and twitch. The movement appeared to cause him great pain, however, because sometimes he grimaced whenever he moved his legs.

"Apakerec?" said the Checrom, who must have been Resita, for his voice sounded the same as the one I had heard in the elevator not more than a couple of minutes ago. "I can't believe it. I didn't think I'd ever see you again."

Something about Resita looked familiar to me, but I was unable to say what. He looked different from the Checrom agents I knew, yet looking at him brought back that same pain in the back of my head that I had felt ever since the Brain Editor healed me when I joined Reunification. I rubbed the back of my head, even though that usually did not help me much whenever I felt that pain.

Resita placed the bowl and wiring down and crawled over to

me. Yea, crawled; despite his functioning legs, he apparently was not strong enough to stand up and walk over to me. Still, he pulled himself along at a quick pace and soon was gripping the bars, his green and brown eyes looking up at me pleadingly.

"Please free me," said Resita. He coughed and hacked before resuming speaking. "Your sword might be able to cut through the bars and—"

"Who are ye again?" I said. "I know not who ye are. I do not even remember ye."

The hope vanished from Resita's eyes as quickly as it had come. "Wait, what? How can you not remember me? We worked together for … well, it was for only about a day, granted, but I thought we became good friends during that time."

"I remember not what ye speak of," I said. "All I know is that I have never seen your face before. Ye are a stranger to me, and nothing more."

"No, I'm not," said Resita, though I detected the hopelessness in his voice easily. "I'm not. Don't you remember the Foundation? How we escaped those lizard creatures through the sewage pipe? And Destroyer, you have to remember the Destroyer."

I quirked an eyebrow. "Lizard creatures? Are ye referring to the Lizard-men? Whilst those creatures are indeed a dangerous bunch, they have never put mine life in jeopardy. As for the Destroyer, that, too, I have managed to avoid, for it is on our side, although I have so rarely seen it around the base."

"How can you not remember any of that?" said Resita. "It was the most dangerous day of my whole life, and yet you forgot it?"

"Assuming it ever even happened as ye say it did," I said. I looked over him at his odd contraption at the back of his cell.

"How did ye access Kiriah's speaker? I was told it was impossible to hack."

"I got desperate," Resita said. "Because I'm usually down here for hours at a time, I spent a good deal of that time trying to get the wires for that speaker. I then used the metal bowl they gave me for my food as a microphone to speak through. It's too complicated to explain."

I frowned. "Whilst I am no expert on audio technology, that seems exceedingly impossible and unlikely to me, albeit quite creative despite that."

"It doesn't matter how I did it," said Resita. He reached through the bars with one of his hands. "Just get me out of here. You can do that, can't you?"

I stepped back out of the reach his hand, which had clipped and stubbed talons. "I am not certain why I would. I know ye not; therefore, I have no reason to aid ye."

"But Reunification is evil," Resita said. "They've been torturing me and interrogating me for … god, I don't even *know* how long because there isn't a clock down here for me to look at."

"Torturing ye?" I said. I snorted. "Impossible. Whilst Reunification does indeed inflict harsh punishments upon those who oppose us, we are not so cold-blooded or wicked as to torture even our enemies."

Resita chuckled, which turned into a hacking cough before it subsided. "Obviously, they haven't told you the *truth*, now have they? Of course not. They don't want you to know how cruel they actually are."

"All ye have done is make baseless accusations against them, bird," I said. That made mine head hurt again, like I had called someone 'bird' before, though I could not remember who. "I see no evidence of torture anywhere."

"You want evidence?" said Resita, his voice much more spiteful now. "*Here* is your evidence."

He turned his head all the way to the right, allowing me to see the left side of his face more fully. It had been partially obscured by the darkness and weak lighting afforded by my skyras sword, but now that he was showing it to me directly, I could barely stomach what I saw.

Four large, thick scars shaped like circles stood out on the left side of his face like unnatural growths. I was no expert on torture, but even I recognized those scars for what they were: signs of a torture method known as four-knife.

'Twas a terrible torture method, it was, and one rarely used by the Knights of Se-Dela. I knew of it only because of my time with the Red Ring Smugglers, for the Smugglers were known for using four-knife to torture rival dealers who tried to sell on their territory. I had never, even as a Smuggler, personally witnessed that, but I had known several Smugglers who were masters at it, and who often spun long tales about the gruesome noises that their victims made as they brought great pain upon them using this method.

As I understood it, the four-knife torture method was done by taking four knives and then cutting a shallow incision in the body of the victim with each knife. Where the incisions were made varied; some made them on their victims' faces, whilst others did it on the chest or back.

What made this method so awful was that it was repeated day in and day out for as long as it took to make the poor victim talk.

And always in the same place; in fact, many practitioners of the four-knife method often carried healing skyras rings as well, which allowed them to heal their victim's cuts so they could cut them afresh the next day.

And each day, they made the incisions slightly deeper and more painful. One of my old Smuggler allies, a dwarf who had known more about the four-knife method than anybody else, had told me that only amateurs cut straight to the bone right away and that the most professional and experienced of torturers would take their sweet time, adding half an inch or less to each incision they made (which would, he had assured me, eventually cut to the bone if the victim in question was strong enough to withstand the pain).

With Resita's scars the way they were, I could tell that whoever had been torturing him must have been an expert. No, not *must have been*, but *was*, for if Resita was telling the truth, then this torture was an ongoing affair. Which meant that the torturer was not done with him yet.

"By the Old Gods," I said, unable to take mine eyes off his scars. "Who did this to ye?"

Resita turned his head so that he was looking at me again, although he now looked even grimmer than before. "Your friends. I don't know their names or even their faces, because they torture me in the dark, but I know that they are Reunification members and always take great delight in making me feel pain."

I blinked several times. "But … this makes no sense. None. Why would my fellow agents torture ye? Does Kiriah know about this? Do the Elders? What about the Founder?"

Resita shrugged. "I don't know for sure, but I'd say that most of the leadership probably does know. They probably even ordered it done."

"Nay," I said, shaking mine head. "This cannot be. We at Reunification are not torturers. We do not inflict such terrible wounds and pain upon anyone, not even upon our enemies. How does that aid us in completing the Mission?"

"They've been torturing me for information," said Resita. He coughed and rubbed the scars on the side of his head. "That's why. I know things that they don't; otherwise, I would be dead already."

"What information could ye possibly know?" I said.

"I am—was—a member of the Foundation," said Resita. "Remember that?"

I nodded. "Yea, I do. They are a wicked organization who have dedicated themselves to stopping our glorious Mission. Though I did not know that we had one of their agents as our prisoners, for I had thought that we had wiped out that organization not long ago."

Resita's eyes widened. "Wiped out? What do you mean by—"

He was interrupted by the *ding* of the elevator. I whipped my head in the direction and saw that the lights above the elevator doors—which showed what floor it was on—were shining. A moment later, the doors opened and a silhouetted being stepped out of it. At first I knew not who it was, until I saw the blinking lights running along the flat of his sword.

"Assassin?" I said, turning to face the robot as the elevator doors closed behind him. "What are ye doing down here?"

A light emitted from Assassin's free hand, though it was rather pointless, seeing as Assassin had no real face to speak of and therefore no eyes with which to see. He had a smooth face plate, which always made me feel uneasy whenever I looked at it, for I could never be certain what this robot was thinking. He may have been a member of Reunification just as I was, but something about his appearance always put me off just the same.

Assassin walked toward me, his sword at his side, as he said, "I was sent here by the Leader to deal with the prisoner. I did not expect to find you down here, although knowing your naivety, perhaps I should have expected it."

I scowled. Assassin always treated me like this. Though he was a robot, he often times acted as though he were better than me. I did not know why he appeared to have some sort of personal vendetta against me, but it mattered not, because at the moment I had more important things to worry about.

"Yea, I spoke with the prisoner," I said, gesturing at Resita's cell. "How long has he been down here? Why was I never told about him? Has Reunification actually been torturing him?"

Assassin stopped. I did not know if he was thinking, but based on his silence, I guessed that he was likely considering what he should tell me. That did make me uncomfortable, for I did not like it when others were not immediately honest with me.

"I do not know the answer to those questions," said Assassin at last. "You will have to ask the Leader. She is in charge of all of our operations, as you very well know. I am nothing more than an individual agent with little knowledge about the overall workings of this organization."

"Yet ye knew about Resita," I pointed out.

"Yes, I did," said Assassin. He pointed back to the elevator doors with his sword. "Now, are you going to stand here and ask me questions I can't answer or are you going to go and speak with the Leader? She's still waiting for you."

I glanced at Resita. Much to my surprise, he was no longer holding his cell's bars; instead, he had retreated to the back of his cell and was curled into a ball. He seemed absolutely terrified, but I did not understand what he could be afraid of until I realized that it 'twas Assassin's voice that had frightened him. That didst make me wonder if Assassin had tortured him.

"Just so you know," said Assassin, interrupting my train of thought and forcing me to look up at him, "the Leader gave me full permission to haul you to her if you won't leave on your own. Despite being your younger sister, she seems to have little problem with bossing you around, I've noticed."

"Kiriah does not boss me around," I said. "But neither will I let you drag me to the pit. I shall go there of mine own free will and get the answers to mine questions there."

Assassin nodded. "So good to see that you *do* have some reason in you after all. And here I thought that you were too curious for your own good."

I ignored his quip, for I was used to them by now. I pressed the tab on my sword's handle and the blade treated into the hilt. Sheathing the sword, I then walked past Assassin, who stepped out of the way to allow me to pass him.

When I reached the elevator doors, I was about to press the button that would take me to the pit when I heard the cell door opening with a loud creaking sound and Resita shouting, "Apakerec! Please don't leave me here with this—"

His words were interrupted the dull sound of metal slapping against flesh and a squawk from Resita, followed by Assassin shouting, "Don't pay any attention to him, Apakerec. He's a liar, like all of the Foundation agents. The Leader needs you right now."

All I wanted to do was turn around and put an end to Assassin. I was not sure why, for I did not know this Resita fellow very well. Besides, if he was indeed an agent of the Foundation, then he deserved whatever Assassin was going to do to him. Even if he died down here, I would show no mercy toward him, for the Founder himself had told me once that to grant mercy to your enemies was to make a mistake that ye would regret for the rest of your life.

Yet still, as I stepped into the elevator, which bounced slightly under mine weight, and then turned around to face the closing doors and feel the elevator rise up, I did not feel any real joy at the thought of what Assassin might do—perhaps continue to do— to Resita.

Chapter Five

Once more, I stepped out of the elevator, only this time, rather than emerge into the dark, dank, and depressing dungeons, I emerged out into the hot night of the Dead Lands.

I had never liked this construction site much; or rather, this dig, for very little had been constructed 'round this large pit aside from the main headquarters and the floodlights that had been built onto the edges of the pit to provide illumination for the workers in the middle of the night. Most of the work, as I understood it, had been in digging out immense amounts of dirt in search of an important part of the Mission. What that part was, no one, not even Kiriah, had told me; even so, I understood that all of this hard work was even more important to the Mission than anything else.

Still, that did not mean I enjoyed it. Day and night, so it seemed to me, were filled with the sounds of workers yelling at each other, drills burrowing deep into the earth, cranes and other heavy machinery dumping the dirt off to the side, and sometimes even explosions shaking mine bed. The explosions were few and far betwixt, but I remember when I first heard them, I had thought that the Old Gods themselves had come down from the moon to destroy us.

Tonight, however, I saw very little of the workers out. The moonlight above showed large drills all set in a neat row several hundred feet from the edge of the pit, while the heavy cranes stood as motionless as rocks. The smell of freshly-dug earth and gun powder filled mine nostrils, but the dig area itself was quieter than usual.

As the elevator doors closed behind me, I looked over mine shoulder at the building behind me. 'Twas the physical headquarters of Reunification's Xeeonite branch, which resembled a rather plain box-shape that I thought was ugly. Oddly, it reminded me of mine family's mansion, although mine family's mansion was a much more beautiful building than this.

Turning away from the building, I noticed one of the workers walking toward me quickly. Like most of the pit diggers, this worker was a dwarf and wore a gray, featureless uniform covered in dirt. Unlike the others, however, his uniform had no sleeves at all, allowing me to see his buff and hairy arms, although there was a line of sweat on his forehead that even I could see in the moonlight from above.

"Apakerec," said the worker as he approached me. "There you are. The Leader told me to go and take you down to meet her in the pit."

I nodded. "Yea, but I believe I can find mine way down there mine self, worker. 'Tis not a difficult thing to use the lift."

"Maybe, but the Leader gave me a mission and I have to do it," said the worker. He turned around and gestured for me to follow. "Come on. Shouldn't take us long to get down there, especially if we move quickly."

Without waiting for mine response, the worker walked away. I followed, but had to walk somewhat slower than I normally did, for mine legs were longer than his and thus mine strides covered more ground with each step. I had to be careful not to overtake him, although he did walk fast for such a short and stout dwarf.

We soon reached the lift, a sort of elevator-like machine built into the wall of the pit to allow workers to travel up and down it with ease. I had never used the machine much, due to the fact that most of mine jobs never took me to the pit, but as I understood it worked similar to the elevator, although 'twas not inclosed.

We stepped onto the lift, which did not shudder under our weight, much to my surprise, although I noticed how dirty the lift 'twas. That made sense, seeing as it was primarily used by the workers, though it was so dirty that I wondered whether it would ever be clean again.

In addition, the lift was high up above the pit. I knew not the pit's exact depth, but when I looked over the railing of the lift, I could not see its bottom, although I did see the white lights strung along the walls, which no doubt provided illumination by which the workers labored. Still, seeing how far above we were, and with only this fragile metal lift to keep us from falling, did make my stomach churn and forced me to step back to avoid getting sick.

When we stepped into the lift, the worker pulled down the metal flat thing in front of the entrance. He then walked over to a lever and pulled it down without another word.

The lift descended into the pit, though it was at a fairly leisurely pace. I mean to say, it went down quickly, and with no delay, but that did not mean that it fell. Even so, I gripped the railing, for I was still not quite used to the feeling of going down on a machine. Did make me feel a little sick, in fact, so I did not look down as we descended in order to keep mine lunch.

As we descended, however, I did pay attention to the walls around us. I noticed other lifts built into the walls, as well as zigzagging paths that appeared to have been dug out by the workers. There were also rooms built into the walls, which had digging equipment such as shovels and drills. No doubt those had been designed to allow the workers to have quicker and easier access to the tools they needed so they wouldst not need to keep going up and down the lift every time they needed something.

The further down we went, the darker it became. Soon, it became so dark that I was unable to see the bearded, bushy face of the worker beside me, who still held the lever down as we went. Soon, however, we passed the string of lights around the walls, which allowed me to see his face again, but even so, the lights were like lights at midnight; they allowed me to see, but shadow still dominated the area like a cruel king.

In another few minutes, the bottom of the pit soon became visible amidst the white lights. The worker began gradually raising the lever, which I did not understand until I noticed our descent slowing to a crawl. Perhaps that was how the lift worked; by altering how much pressure the dwarf put on it, he could control how quickly or how slowly we descended.

And then the lift finally touched the bottom of the pit floor. As soon as it did, the worker let go of the lever and pushed open the metal guardrail that acted as the lift's entrance. He then stepped aside and gestured at me to go first. "Go on. Just keep walking straight and turn down the first tunnel to your right. The Leader will be down there."

I nodded. "Thank ye for your help."

I then stepped off the lift. As soon as I did, the worker closed the guardrail and the lift immediately rose back up. I looked up after it, wondering why it was leaving so quickly and why the worker did not stay to get us out of here after our meeting. Perhaps the worker had important work to do or maybe there was another way out of here that we could take, although I did not know for certain.

In any case, I turned and began walking across the rocky and uneven ground of the pit. 'Twas quite a bit cooler down here than it was on the pit's rim, likely because it was so far from the hot surface of the Dead Lands. I still smelt dirt and gun powder, however, which was hardly a pleasant scent, though I did my best to ignore it anyway.

Wherever I looked, I saw the large, massive drills and carts full of dirt and dug-up rock. Huge piles of dirt dwarfed me, with some pickaxes, shovels, and other equipment stabbed into them, likely left here by the workers so they could have quick and easy access to their tools when they returned from their breaks.

But so far as mine eyes could tell, there were no workers down here at all. Granted, they were probably on break, but it still made me feel more than a little afraid. I had no reason to fear, of course, for there was nothing remotely dangerous or lethal in this pit; still, I would have felt better if the workers had been digging and hauling dirt all around me. The silence 'twas unnerving.

Soon, I noticed the entrance to the tunnel that the worker told me of. This tunnel did slope underground, which appeared to actually go 'neath the floor of the pit itself. Did make me wonder how much father I would need to go down, although I decided not to question it and simply find out on mine own.

So I walked down into the tunnel, which was indeed quite a bit darker and narrower than the pit itself. The ceiling, too, was lower, forcing me to bend over slightly to keep from scraping mine scalp against it. Clearly, the dwarves had not dug out this place with the intention of humans or some other taller species using it, which bothered me, although I said nothing about it, for there 'twas no one to complain to.

Thankfully, this tunnel was not very long. Up ahead, I saw a bright light, which prompted me to speed up mine progress. I heard voices speaking up ahead, one of which was clearly Kiriah's, but the others were mixed together, which made it difficult for me to determine who they were. That did puzzle me, however, because I had thought that it would only be me and Kiriah down here today. Had she invited others to be a part of our conversation? If so, who were they?

Soon, I emerged into a much larger room than the tunnel, allowing me to stand up to mine full height. Mine eyes took a second to adjust to the change in brightness, but when they did, I could quite clearly see the room in which I had emerged.

'Twas not a large room, that was for certain. It was perhaps half as wide as the room in which Sura had been held hostage by those foul Smugglers, and smelled like freshly dug dirt. There were odd carvings and pictures along the walls, which looked ancient to me, but they were too faded for me to make out perfectly. A single light bulb hung from the ceiling, which offered the only illumination in the place.

And of course, I was not alone. Mine sister Kiriah, with her blonde hair and red robes, stood near the center, speaking with three other beings. One of them was human, the other a Jikorian, and still another a Checrom. I at first did not recognize them until I remembered who they were: The Elders of Reunification.

The Elders were six of the leaders of Reunification. They were above Kiriah, but below the Founder. Half of them were on Xeeo, where they helped oversee the operations of the Xeeonite branch, whilst the other half were on Dela and oversaw the operations there. I rarely interacted with the Elders, for they were too far above me in the chain of command to ever associate with me; still, every member of Reunification knew who they were and always treated them with the utmost respect that they deserved. After all, they had been appointed by the Founder himself for their wisdom and ability, which meant that they were indeed a cut above the rest of us.

I even knew the names of these three elders. The human was Xarna, a round, fat man who had a single ponytail hanging from the back of his bald head; the Jikorian was Moka, a female who to my knowledge never spoke even when in meeting with the rest of the Elders; and the third and final was Arita, a female Checrom with red feathers and sharp gray eyes.

When I saw Arita, I was reminded of Resita, even though the two Checrom hardly looked alike. In mine mind's eye, I saw his weak, naked body curled up against the back wall of his cell, but I did away with that mental image, for it was hardly important to mine current situation. All it did was distract, and it would not do for me to be distracted in this situation.

I did not even have to announce my presence to be noticed, for Kiriah glanced in my direction when I entered and a large smile spread across her face. She then said, "Rii!" and ran over and hugged me tightly. I hugged her back and then she let go and stepped away, whilst the Elders merely turned to look at me, although that was fine, for if they had hugged me as well, that would have indeed been quite awkward.

"I am glad you got here," said Kiriah, putting her hands together eagerly. "I thought you were never going to get here."

"Yes, well, I was a bit distracted, as ye know," I said. "I went and spoke with Resita, that Foundation agent we have kept imprisoned under the headquarters. The one ye never told me about."

Kiriah's smile vanished as quickly as it came, replaced by an alarmed frown, as though I had mentioned a dark secret I was not supposed to know about. "Oh, well, I'm sorry for not telling you about him. It's just that, well, I didn't think you needed to know about him. He would have been a distraction from your job, which is to help bring about the completion of the Mission in whatever ways you can."

"Yea, I agree," I said. "But Resita claimed that I knew him once, even though I do not remember him at all."

Kiriah laughed, although something about her laughter did not seem genuine to me. "That's because he's a liar, Rii. If he said he knew you, it was because he was trying to deceive you into helping him escape. You know how deceptive and wicked the Foundation is."

I stroked my chin. "Yea, I do indeed. I suppose ye are probably right. I should not have let his words get to me. But I still do not understand why we have apparently been torturing him."

Kiriah's laughter immediately died away. She looked as though I had said a terrible insult, one she was not ready to respond to. I knew not what was so shocking or offensive about what I said, but perhaps even she had not known about the torture that I had seen proof of.

It was Arita who stepped forward and said, "The Foundation agent known as Resita deserves the interrogation techniques we use on him. While Reunification does not like to use such harsh methods to extract information from our enemies, I dearly hope that you are not suggesting that this wicked villain, who has tried to block the progress of the Mission before, is undeserving of such just punishment?"

Arita looked at me with the most judging and questioning of gazes that I could say nothing more than, "Well, of course not. I said not that I thought he was undeserving of it—all enemies of Reunification deserve nothing less than the harshest of punishments for their opposition to our noble cause—but I found it odd that no one had told me about this, Elder, not even once."

I chose mine words carefully, for I did not wish to offend Arita or any of the other Elders. To offend the Elders was a great crime in Reunification; indeed, it was so heavily discouraged that I knew not of even one instance of any of my fellow agents doing so. Only the Founder himself commanded more respect than they.

"That is because you do not hold a high ranking in Reunification, Apakerec," said Arita, her words cold. "You are allowed to know only as much as we think you should know, and nothing more."

"I understand that, Elder," I said. "I apologize for going and speaking with the prisoner. I shall not do it again."

"Good," said Arita. "The next time you see the prisoner will be when we *tell* you to see him. Understood?"

I nodded without hesitation, although in truth, I still wondered about Resita. I did not like the idea of torturing even one of our enemies, but I also knew better than to openly contradict an Elder. 'Twas better to make her think I agreed with her than to come out and voice mine disagreement with her. I would likely have been given a terrible punishment for mine disagreement, no matter how respectful I phrased it.

"How is Sura?" asked Kiriah, drawing mine attention back to her. "Is he all right?"

"Nay," I said, shaking mine head. "He was attacked by the Smugglers. They took him hostage and attempted to use his life to take mine own. I healed him as best as I could, but methinks he needs to see a qualified doctor to ensure that he heals well."

"How horrible," said Kiriah. "How did you defeat them?"

For the brief second before I answered her question, I considered whether or not to tell her about Sura's strange and mysterious new powers. Did seem an important thing to mention; however, I was not certain that I wanted the Elders to know about it. Whilst I did not distrust the Elders, necessarily, I decided that they did not need to know about this right now. Perhaps I would tell them later.

"With great effort, sister," I said, with as much gusto as I could. "The curs fell before mine awesome might. And they fled and will likely never bother another member of our family ever again."

"Wonderful," said Kiriah with a smile. "I knew you could stop them, Rii. But what about Sura?"

"Our older brother was still injured by them, sadly," I said with a sigh, running my hand through my hair. "I had to spirit him away from our mansion, especially when the Knights of Se-Dela came a-knocking and tried to arrest me. When I came here, however, I brought Sura with me and gave him to Arn and Lauz to deliver to the medical room so his injuries could be treated."

"How did you get away from the Knights?" asked Kiriah.

"Through mine wits and ingenuity, of course," I said. "Still, our mansion is not a safe place to return to. I imagine that the Knights are likely going to keep an eye on it in case of our return. I suggest, therefore, that we stay away from it for now."

Kiriah's shoulders slumped. "Aw. I was hoping I'd get to go back there soon, but I guess I'll have to put off that visit for later."

"I understand your disappointment, sister, but fear not," I sad. I put a hand on her shoulder, causing her to look at me in the eyes. "Once the Mission is complete, then we will be able to return to our home and live there forever, if ye like."

Kiriah smiled. "Yeah, you're right. That just gives us an even greater incentive to complete the Mission, doesn't it?"

"Indeed it does," I said. "Now, why did ye summon me down here? 'Tis a strange place to have an important meeting."

"Because there's something I want to show you," said Kiriah. "Something very important."

She stepped aside, as did the Elders, now allowing me to see for myself the thing that they had stood in front of.

Protruding from the earth was a sharp rock; nay, not just a rock, but a carved one, like a master mason had created it. The rock was a pale green and still covered partially in dirt, but I could tell that it had at one point been a beautiful piece of art, and perhaps still would be, if we dug it up and cleaned it.

But I did not understand its significance, for it seemed not to me to be very special. Although I did notice how large it was; the rest of it, which was buried 'neath our feet, was likely enormous, perhaps twice as large as the full moon statue back at our mansion, if not even larger than that.

"What is it?" I asked, looking at Kiriah in curiosity. "Does it have something to do with the Mission?"

"Bingo," said Kiriah. "That rock is an important part of the puzzle; in fact, it is *the* most important part. It is what we have been looking for ever since we began digging in this spot."

"That is indeed important," I said. "But that still does not explain perfectly what this thing is, exactly."

"It is a Unification Stone," said Arita, causing me to look at her. She and the other Elders had been so quiet I had almost forgotten about them. "One of two. The other is in Dela, which is what our Delanian agents over there have been searching for."

"Unification Stone?" I said. "I have never heard of that."

"Not surprising," said Arita. "Few have, outside of Reunification and the Foundation. Especially with only two of them in existence."

"What does a Unification Stone do, exactly?" I asked.

"That is simple," said Arita. She walked up to the protruding Stone and rubbed one of her feathery hands against it. "Ages ago, when Dela and Xeeo were one world, they were held together by a magical rock known as the Unity Rock. The Unity Rock held the worlds together by constantly generating skyras energy. Think of it like a giant magnet, and skyras energy as magnetic waves that held together the two halves that would become Dela and

Xeeo."

"Oh," I said. "So it has a twin on Dela, then. But how did the Unity Rock split?"

"That is what caused the one world to become two," said Arita. "The Unity Rock was split, and as a result, Dela and Xeeo were born. None of us know how the split occurred, save for the Founder, who was there to witness it when it happened."

"It doesn't matter how it was split, anyway," Xarna spoke up, waving off the question like it was an annoying bug. "What matters is that we have now found one half of the Unity Rock. We have been searching for decades for the location of Xeeo's Unification Stone and now that we have found it, we are so close to completing the Mission that I can practically taste it."

"This is indeed something worth celebrating," I said. "What might our next move be? Is there some way we can fuse the worlds together again?"

"Not right away," said Kiriah. "I wish to the Old Gods that we could, but we still need to dig up the Unification Stone in its entirety before we can do anything with it. At the moment, that means we have to leave it here, but our workers are going to be working harder than ever to extract it from the earth, so it should be completely unearthed before long."

"This is wondrous news of the highest order," I said. "What about our Delanian brothers? Have they found Dela's Unification Stone yet?"

"They have," said Kiriah. "Kalcan told me that they're still digging it out, just like what we're doing here, but unfortunately, the Foundation's assault on the pit there forced them to put off the dig for a while."

I nodded. I remembered hearing about that assault, for it had happened roughly around the same time when I joined Reunification. From what I heard, two agents of the Foundation— one a witch, the other a robot, perhaps the only two survivors from our attack on their Delanian branch—had assaulted our Delanian brothers. They knocked over one of our cranes onto the main building of that site, which had killed a dozen workers, as well as killing Juya and Lamos, two of the three Delanian Elders. Whilst Kalcan had succeeded in killing the witch, the robot had gotten away and no one had seen him since.

"But Kalcan told me that he is working his workers harder than ever to dig out the Delanian Unification Stone as fast as possible," said Kiriah, rubbing her hands together in excitement. "He says they'll have their Stone unearthed in no time."

"That is amazing," I said. "And wonderful. It appears to me that there is nothing that can stop us now."

"I know," said Kiriah. "Soon, everything will be as it should be. The worlds will be healed, like the Founder always says. Won't that be great?"

I was about to agree, but at that moment, the echoes of heavy footsteps came from the tunnel. That sound did make me look over mine shoulder, wondering who was coming. They were running so fast that it sounded as though they were trying to get away from something that chased them, although I knew of nothing down here that would do that.

A moment later, one of the dwarfish workers dashed in. He was panting hard, putting his hands on his small knees, his face covered in sweat. He appeared to have run for a long time, although why he had run I did not know.

111

"Worker?" I said. "What are ye doing here? Do ye have important news for us?"

"Yes," said the worker in between gasps for air. "Extremely … important. Just heard it a few minutes ago. Came down here as fast as I could to tell all of you. Hugely important."

"Well, spit it out," Arita snapped. "Don't just stand there and look like an idiot. Tell us what it is."

The dwarf looked up at us, the urgency in his eyes making me a bit fearful, and said, "It's Xacron-Ah. He's … been kidnapped by the remaining Foundation agents. And they want to make a deal with us in exchange for his freedom."

Chapter Six

We followed the dwarf out of the tunnel and onto the nearest lift, which was wider and larger than the lift I had originally taken down here. The dwarf pulled the lever up and soon we were rising much faster than I had descended, the bottom of the pit rapidly fading into the darkness as we drew closer to the surface above.

None of us spoke a word as we ascended, likely because the situation was indeed quite tense for us. I took advantage of this moment to think about Xacron-Ah, even though I usually did not think too much about him due to the fact that he and I were not the best of friends and had never interacted much.

Xacron-Ah was one of our agents, who, unlike the rest of us, acted in the public as the Mayor of the city of Xeeon, a city which, whilst hardly next door, 'twas not terribly far from our current base. Far enough that no one could find us accidentally, but not far enough that the distance was insurmountable for us to cross if necessary.

Xacron-Ah's job within Reunification 'twas simple. He used his political power as Xeeon's Mayor to keep as many people out of the Dead Lands as possible to avoid people outside of our organization from stumbling upon our operations here. That was what Kiriah had explained to me; and indeed, Xacron-Ah had done a good job of using his political powers to install heavy fines and taxes for anyone who wished to travel to the Dead Lands from Xeeon. I had even heard that he had managed to convince the other Xeeonite cities along the Dead Lands' border to prevent others from coming down here as well, although I knew not how he had accomplished that, for the cities of Xeeo were quite independent and rarely got along, or so I understood from what Kiriah and others had told me (not having lived here long, I had to trust they were telling me the truth).

That Xacron-Ah had been kidnapped, however, was an exceedingly terrifying idea. Moreover, that he had been kidnapped by the remaining agents of the Foundation was even more worrying. And that they wanted to make a deal with us … oh, that worried me greatly, and I was no great worrier most of the time.

In a few more minutes, we reached the top of the pit, left the lift, and entered the main building. Here we took one of the teleporters built into the headquarters, which took us directly to the command center.

The headquarters' command center 'twas a large room, possibly the largest in all of the building. It had dozens of computer monitors, displaying things such as the *Xeeon Daily News Channel*, weather forecast for the Dead Lands, reports from Reunification agents in the field on their activities, and so on. The room was a cooler temperature than the outside, although it had no discernible or distinct smell to speak of; a common feature of Xeeonite buildings, for they were usually scrubbed clean in ways I knew not.

There were no people in this room; from what I understood,

most of the work in here was entirely automated. Only one person —the dwarf who had alerted us of this news earlier—was in here at any one time, and then only to monitor the machines and ensure that they were all functioning correctly.

I rarely came to this room, for I usually had no need to; besides, all of the computer monitors—some of which floated and flew around the room at will, and some of which were built into the walls—confused me and made me highly uncomfortable. That feeling of confusion did return when we teleported into the room, but I soon forgot about it when I noticed the largest screen of all, which was on the back wall, visible no matter where ye stood in the command center.

On the screen 'twas a woman I had never seen before. She was probably human and wore silver robes that hid her swollen back. She was not exactly an ugly woman, but I found myself put off by her appearance nonetheless, perhaps because she was staring at us severely through the monitor. Something about her appearance reminded me about the Founder—likely the eyes, for her eyes did remind me of the Founder, being even the same shade of blue. 'Twas likely a coincidence, however, because the Founder never mentioned having a sister or female relative of any sort before.

Kiriah stepped forward, showing much bravery in the face of this strange woman, and said, "Who are you?"

The woman did not smile or show any sort of amusement. "I wish to speak with the Founder, not you or the Elders."

Kiriah folded her arms. "Sorry, but I am Kiriah, the Leader of Reunification. Negotiating with enemies is one of my duties."

"I don't care what your duties are," said the woman. I heard the sound of someone gagging off-screen, though who that might be, I knew not. "My agents and I specifically kidnapped Xacron-Ah in order to secure a screen meeting with the Founder. Where is he?"

"He's busy," said Kiriah. "But I can take a message for him, if you'd like."

The woman's brows furrowed. "I am not an idiot, Kiriah. Whatever the Founder is doing can't be more important than talking to me."

"Actually, it is," said Kiriah. "Why don't you just tell us your name already? I don't even know who you are."

The woman sighed. "Fine. I'm the Head of the Foundation. I presume you've heard of me?"

I had to stifle a gasp when I heard that name. I had been told about the Head once, but I had not known that she had survived the army of Lizard-men that we had sent to the Foundation's Delanian branch. Reports had indicated that the Head was dead and that only a handful of agents had survived the slaughter; now, however, it was clear that she was alive, well, and demanding to speak with the Founder, which did make me exceedingly uncomfortable.

Kiriah tried not to show any signs of shock, but I knew mine sister well enough to read her body language, especially when she unfolded her arms. Though she stood her ground, she did scratch the side of her neck, which 'twas one of her ways of showing she was surprised.

"So you survived our attack on your Delanian base," said Kiriah. "Interesting. I thought for sure you had died."

"Did you honestly believe that I would die in that attack?" said the Head. "I guess, if you thought *that*, the Founder must not have told you very much about me, did he?"

"It doesn't matter," said Kiriah, waving that off, though I could easily tell that mine sister was indeed disturbed by this particular revelation. "Where is Xacron-Ah? I don't see him anywhere."

"He's currently to my left, just off-screen," said the Head. "But I suppose it wouldn't do any harm to show him. J997, please bring our captive on screen."

I heard more grunting and dragging, and the next moment Xacron-Ah's large face appeared on screen. He did not look as if he had been terribly mistreated, although there were bruises on his face and his left orange eye was swollen slightly. A gag had been stuffed into his mouth, some kind of rubber ball from what I could tell, that did nothing to hide the pleading in his eyes for us to save him as plain as day.

Then his face was pulled off-screen again and the Head reappeared, looking as disapproving as ever.

"So you see, we're not bluffing when we say that we have him," said the Head. "In fact, that is how we are contacting you at all. We are using his com-watch to connect with your computers, as you no doubt already know."

"Very well," said Kiriah. "I believe you. I can see that you have Xacron-Ah and will hurt him if you don't get what you want from us."

"More or less," said the Head. "Now that we have that out of the way, I demand to speak with the Founder. I don't care about small-fry like you or those three Elders behind your back. What I care about is talking to your true leader."

"As I said before, he is not available," said Kiriah. "If you want to deal with us, you have to speak with me. It's not exactly a complicated concept for you to wrap your head around, you know."

The Head sighed heavily. "Fine. Although I wonder if the Founder simply does not want to talk to me because he doesn't want to see me again."

"And what does that mean?" said Kiriah. "Do you know the Founder?"

"We've met before," said the Head in a vague way. "But that is irrelevant to the discussion. Let's start our deal."

The Head's comment—'We've met before'—did interest me, because I had not known that the Founder and the Head had once known each other. Of course, being the leaders and founders of two ancient organizations that had been fighting each other in the shadows of secrecy for many years, perhaps 'twas no surprise that they happened to be acquainted. I did wonder, though, what circumstances their previous meeting had been under.

"All right," said Kiriah. "What do you want from us?"

"Simple," said the Head. "In exchange for Xacron-Ah, I want you to cease all operations on both Dela and Xeeo. You will then disband Reunification and stop trying to reunite the two worlds."

"Utterly ridiculous," Arita said, before Kiriah could respond. "Xacron-Ah is a valuable agent, but he is not that valuable. We will not cease our operations on both worlds just to get one agent back."

"Are you certain?" said the Head. She smiled in an amused sort of way that made my spine tingle with fear. "If that's your final answer, I suppose that's your right. As for us, we'll just take Xacron-Ah's personal files and distribute them to the Xeeonite

118

and Delanian governments, which will of course reveal your existence and your plans to everyone, which I think would make it a great deal harder for you to complete your precious Mission, wouldn't you say?"

Kiriah stepped forward this time, her eyes fixed squarely on the Head's smug and arrogant smile. "You wouldn't."

The Head shrugged. "I don't have any reason not to. While I would prefer to keep our conflict a secret, I also realize that Reunification is not equipped to deal with the combined might of the Xeeonite *and* Delanian governments, even if you have agents on the inside of both groups. I can't imagine that the United Federation of Xeeonite Nations or the Mystical Alliance of Dela would be happy to learn that you are trying to take both of their worlds out of existence."

I gulped, for I knew about both of those planetary alliances. Many, many nations on both worlds were allied with one of those organizations. They technically lacked any real political power over individual groups, but that mattered little, because if they did indeed find out about Reunification, I could see the two organizations banding together to squash us from existence. Both organizations represented billions of people; indeed, even the Old Gods may be unable to save us from that power.

But I said nothing, for I knew that negotiating with enemies was part of Kiriah's job. I trusted that mine sister would be able to come up with a way to secure our future, although I knew not what, for the Head did not seem very likely to settle for anything less than what she had already demanded of us.

"So as you can see," said the Head, "it is obvious who has the power in this negotiation. If you agree to our demands, we will let

Xacron-Ah go free. We might not even tell the authorities about your illegal activities on both worlds. Everyone can return to their normal lives without ever having to answer for their crimes."

I looked at Kiriah. I wondered what she was thinking. Even though I knew her body language well, at the moment it was difficult to read. She was probably thinking about how to get out of this situation, but the longer she stood there in silence, the more I began to worry that she might not know how to negotiate this deal in our favor at all.

"Well?" said the Head. "I am awaiting your answer, Kiriah. Either cease operations and hand the Founder over to us, or get ready to face the public."

Kiriah bit her lower lip. She glanced in the direction of one of the floating monitors, which immediately turned away from her, though I did not understand what that meant or if it meant anything at all.

Then Kiriah brushed her bangs off her forehead and said, "So this is your deal, is it? Force us to end our operations or else expose us to the peoples of the two worlds, which would do the same thing, more or less."

"Exactly," said the Head. "Again, what is your answer? Will you accept it or reject it?"

'Twas a hard situation. The Elders and I looked at Kiriah expectantly. She was silent now; indeed, I wondered if the pressure of the situation had taken away her ability to speak. After all, this was quite a stressful situation, for either way, this would not work out well in our favor. I prayed to the Old Gods to provide Kiriah with the wisdom and insight she needed to overcome this ordeal.

Finally, Kiriah said, "Head, you didn't honestly expect us to fall for that, did you?"

She spoke with such confidence that even I was stunned. Even the Head looked surprised, though to tell ye the truth, she looked more confused than anything.

"What?" said the Head. "What do you mean? This is not some trickery or deception on our part. We actually do have Xacron-Ah. You saw him yourself."

"I saw that," said Kiriah. "But you seem to think that you have us in a bind, when in truth, you don't."

"You're bluffing," said the Head. "I can see through your false confidence."

"False confidence?" said Kiriah. She gestured at herself. "This is all one hundred percent real here."

"I don't understand," said the Head. "There is clearly no way out of this situation that will end well for you. Though nice try with your attempt to convince me that your confidence is real; all I see is a weak attempt at bluffing."

"Believe what you want about my confidence, but the fact is, this is not as sticky a situation as you are trying to make it out to be," said Kiriah. She folded her arms over her chest once more, looking as commanding an authority as any leader I knew. "So you think that you can distribute Xacron-Ah's files to the public, thus revealing our existence to the worlds."

"Exactly," said the Head. "We have already established this. I don't see why you need to repeat it."

Kiriah gestured at one of the floating monitors, the one I had seen her glance at before, which zoomed over to her and floated next to her head immediately. "Because I've already deleted those files from his com-watch."

I could not see the floating monitor, nor what was upon its face, but I could see the Head's reaction. She leaned forward, her face becoming even larger on the monitor, an expression of disbelief and horror appearing on her features. 'Twas a satisfying thing to see, indeed.

"But … how?" said the Head. I found great satisfaction in the confusion in her voice. "I did not even realize you were doing it."

"Xacron-Ah's com-watch is connected to our headquarters' systems," said Kiriah. "As a result, our computers have access to the files stored on it. While you talked, I had one of our computers go in and delete every last file on his com-watch. Now you have nothing to show to anyone and nothing to use against us."

What a brilliant move. In one fell swoop, mine sister had not only successfully denied the Head and her cronies their satisfaction, but had ensured that the Mission would continue on unabated. It did make me proud of my younger sister, for I now saw in her a much more intelligent and savvy woman than I had known existed.

The Head pulled back, looking as defeated and bamboozled as if a trained boxer had punched her in the face. "I … this can't be …"

"But it is," said Kiriah. She patted the floating monitor beside her. "You can see the proof for yourself on the monitor. Xac's com-watch is good only for contacting us now, but of course that is not what you need it for, right?"

Even the Elders were looking at Kiriah with more respect than I had ever seen them view her with before. That did not surprise me, however, because mine sister was indeed the smartest and savviest woman in all of the two worlds. I wished I could be as smart and clever as her, though I did not envy her, for I did not wish for envy to ruin our relationship.

'Twas the greatest victory for Reunification I had yet witnessed. Indeed, it was so great that I was absolutely certain now that there was nothing that could stop us. The Foundation was too weak and scattered to be of much use against us, even with Xacron-Ah as their hostage; the governments and peoples of the worlds did not even know we existed; and the Unification Stones were within our grasp. I saw no way that anyone could stop the glorious Mission. Praise be to the Old Gods!

"Now," said Kiriah, "I think we are done negotiating with you fools. We have some very important business to attend to, you see, and I just don't have the time to waste talking to a toothless tiger like you anymore."

Kiriah raised her hand, likely to shut off the monitor, before an off-screen voice—metallic, mechanical, and rather dull—said, "Head, I have ascertained the coordinates and location of Reunification's headquarters in the Dead Lands. I have now sent these coordinates to the Database, which the government of Xeeon will also receive shortly."

Without warning, the Head's smile returned. She looked at whoever just said that and said, "Thank you, J997. I appreciate the effort. Have you received a response yet?"

"None," said the voice, which undoubtedly belonged to this villainous 'J997,' whoever he was. "But anonymous tips are rarely responded to. Most likely, the Database will send out a squadron of J bots to investigate the claim. Once they have determined that the claim has a basis in fact, I imagine they'll send an entire special forces team to take control of the base and arrest any Reunification agents they can find, maybe even a small army, because I made sure to include not only the base's location, but its size and number of residents, which was also included with the rest of its data."

"Wonderful," said the Head. She then turned to look at us again. "How did you like my acting? I tried to look as devastated as I could, in order to make you think that your little revelation had actually set us back. Of course it didn't. Because you see, Kiriah, I have decided to repay in kind for your slaughtering my agents. Let's see how long you last when the government of Xeeon decides to attack you."

Now it was mine sister's turn to look astonished. She did not even seem able to speak, which caused righteous anger to flow through mine body, for I hated seeing anyone treat mine sister in that way.

I stepped forward and pointed at the Head's evil face on the screen. "Ye cur and wench, how dare ye do this! Ye are nothing but the scum of the earth, the dirt between the toes of the giants, a blight on the universe. Once I see ye in person, I will make ye wish that ye had never been born, ye monster."

The Head looked at me in amusement. "I've never been called a wench before, but it doesn't really matter. Soon, all of you will be behind bars or hiding in the dirt like the rats you are. Meanwhile, we will be sitting here, laughing at your agony. Tell the Founder I said hello."

Then the screen went as blank as a virgin piece of paper. We all stared at the screen for perhaps thirty seconds, although it seemed like the longest thirty seconds of mine life.

Chapter Seven

Then Kiriah shook her head and turned to face us. Dread and panic shadowed her face and she shook where she stood; 'twas the first time I had seen mine sister so fearful and worried.

"We have to tell the Founder and everyone else," said Kiriah. "Immediately. Where is he?"

"In his quarters," said Arita. She made a disturbed chirping sound. "We need to contact Kalcan and the others on Dela. If the Xeeonites will be coming after us, they will inevitably learn of our Delanian brothers as well. Our brothers must be informed so they will not be caught."

"I will go and tell the Founder myself," said Kiriah. "You can contact our Delanian brothers. Tell them what happened and that we will be contacting them again with instructions from the Founder shortly."

The Elders nodded and ran to the teleporter. I watched them vanish instantly upon stepping on it, causing me to turn to face Kiriah, who looked more troubled than I had seen her look in some time.

"What am I supposed to do, Kiriah?" I asked. "May I track down this vile woman and teach her a lesson in harming our plans?"

"No," said Kiriah, shaking her head. "While I'd love to go and teach that witch a lesson, we don't know where she is, and even if we did, going after her would be dangerous. The Head is far more powerful than you think."

"What shall I do, then?" I said.

"Come with me," said Kiriah. "We need to find the Founder and tell him about what happened. I want you to be with me because … well, I think you know why."

I understood. Kiriah looked so scared and helpless that I doubted she would be able to speak very reasonably or understandably to anyone right now. As her older brother, 'twas my job to support her however I could, a job I did gladly.

Hence, we dashed over to the teleporter. The holographic keyboard appeared on it and Kiriah quickly typed in the four digit number of the Founder's quarters.

'Twas an instant later that the command center vanished around us and we found ourselves standing in a room I had never visited before (though 'twas one I had heard much about). It was a large room, with half of it made of rock and the other half made of metal, a perfect balance betwixt the two materials that looked odd to me, although I questioned it not, for I knew that the Founder often loved to mix things that did not always seem to go together.

The room did smell of a strange scent, like oranges, although I knew not why. The room was empty, save for the teleporter, and at the end of it, there was a closed door, which was the door to the Founder's room. We dashed 'cross the room as fast as we could, but Kiriah reached it first and knocked on the door hard. I normally would have told her to knock on it more gently, but considering how urgent the situation was, I did not tell her to hold back.

"Founder!" Kiriah shouted. "Founder! Please answer! We have an urgent message to deliver to you. Something horrible has happened and—"

Without warning, the door swung open inwards. Kiriah immediately stopped beating on it and the two us stepped back, although there was no one in the doorway at first. All I saw was the darkness of the room beyond, which made me wonder for a moment if the Founder did not have electricity in his room.

A moment later, however, the Founder himself appeared in the doorway. He did look the same as always; a face that was half-organic, half-mechanical, a sight I always found unsettling, despite respecting the Founder more than anyone else I knew. He wore the same golden wizard's robes as he always did, his mechanical hands peeking out from the sleeves. His dual eye colors—left one, an organic blue, the right, an artificial red—also did seem exceedingly unnatural to me, though I said not a word about it to his face so as to avoid offending him.

"What is the problem, Kiriah?" said the Founder. Despite the urgency of the situation, he spoke quite calmly and did not seem annoyed by our interrupting him. "What is the situation? It sounds urgent."

"It *is* urgent," said Kiriah. She spoke so fast that she was almost incomprehensible. "The Head just contacted us. The Foundation kidnapped Xacron-Ah and the Head has threatened to distribute his files to the Xeeonites and Delanians to expose us to the world but we deleted them but then she had one of her cronies send the coordinates of our location to the Database and now—"

The Founder held up one hand. 'Twas a simple gesture, but it caused Kiriah to quiet immediately. It also filled me with calmness, as the Founder's presence and actions always did, even though I was not as upset or terrified as Kiriah.

"Slow down," said the Founder, his tone as gentle as a father's is to his daughter. "Start at the beginning. What happened?"

Kiriah took a deep breath and started again. She explained all that had happened within the last ten minutes or so (although it had seemed like hours to me), whilst the Founder listened without a sound. He was so still that it was eerie, for I had never seen anyone stand so still, save for the robots I had seen in Xeeon when I arrived in Xeeo two and a half weeks ago.

When Kiriah finished recounting the recent events, the Founder looked deeply troubled.

"So the Head has finally decided to strike the decisive blow against us," said the Founder. He did not sound troubled at all, even though this was an awful turn of events that I did not think we had much of a chance of recovering from. "We must have pushed her to the brink, after destroying both of their bases."

"What are we going to do?" asked Kiriah. "If we abandon the base, then that means abandoning the Unification Stone, which means abandoning the—"

"We will *never* abandon the Mission," said the Founder, cutting her off. He spoke with such severity that I was surprised, for he was usually very calm. "Never. Do not even suggest—no, do not even *think*—such a vile thought. The worlds are hurting and broken. They need our help, even if they do not know it."

Kiriah bit her lower lip. "Sorry, Founder. I was just so

frightened that I didn't know what to say."

"I understand, Kiriah, but you must also understand that when we dedicate our lives to the Mission, then we *will* complete the Mission, regardless of what obstacles stand in our way," said the Founder. He put a hand on his chest. "It is our destiny to heal the worlds, which have been split so long. You cannot abandon your destiny. You can run from it, try to deny it, but sooner or later, it will catch up with you. And once it does, it will destroy you."

"Indeed," I said, nodding in agreement. "But Founder, that still does not explain what we need to do. Once the J bots discover what we are up to, they will undoubtedly overrun this place and arrest every last one of us."

The Founder stroked his chin. Whilst I appreciated the Founder's general calmness in this stressful situation, I found it bothersome how he seemed not at all concerned about our current problems. Every minute we stood here, contemplating the issue, was another minute wasted not acting on the issue, and this bothered me, for action was the only way to solve anything.

Finally, the Founder lowered his hand and said, in his usual calm voice, "This changes nothing."

'Twas shocked to my core when I heard that. So was Kiriah, who looked like she had been slapped in the face by the Founder's words.

"What?" said Kiriah, blinking rapidly as she looked at the Founder. "But … what …"

"While I appreciate you informing me of this turn of events, I do not believe that we must change tactics or abandon the Mission, which is what the Head is hoping for," said the Founder. "Instead, we will increase the speed at which we are digging out the Unification Stones. Get *all* workers back on the Unification Stone immediately. Every last one of them. Send a message to Kalcan on Dela to push his workers as well."

Kiriah looked so taken aback by this that she seemed to be at a loss for words. That I understood, for I, too, had a hard time seeing the logic in this pronouncement, as it appeared to me to be exceedingly foolish in light of recent events.

Indeed, I thought it so foolish that I said, in the most respectful voice I could muster in the current situation, "Sir, whilst I am in no way at all whatsoever trying to suggest that we *abandon* the Mission, I do think that perhaps we ought to put it off until later. I mean to say that it will likely be within the day that the J bots arrive, and when they do, I doubt they will have much trouble in arresting us, for those machines are indeed quite good at what they were designed to do."

I chose each word carefully; I was no wordsmith nor storyteller, but I could at least make sure that the Founder did not mistake my opposition for insubordination.

But then the Founder lashed out with his hand and grabbed mine neck. His metallic fingers were cold against mine skin and he raised me up, causing me to hack and choke under his powerful grip. I could not even speak, but I could look down on the Founder, whose eyes were blazing with anger at me.

"The Mission must be completed," said the Founder. All of the calmness in his voice had evaporated; 'twas as though it hadn't been there at all. "It *must* be. We are so close to healing the worlds. But if you continue to question my orders, then I am afraid you will not live long enough to see the glorious day that the old world—*my* home—is brought back."

His grip tightened around mine neck, choking me even more. I could feel the air leaving mine lungs, feel unconsciousness beginning to come over me, but I was unable to tell him to stop, to tell him that I still supported the Mission. It appeared that the Founder was so enraged at my doubtful words that he was going to kill me anyway, for I saw no gentleness or kindness in his eyes anymore.

But then Kiriah reached out and grabbed his arm. That caused the Founder's grip on mine neck to loosen slightly and allow some air to flow through mine lungs, although 'twas still horribly painful and I could barely think much less breathe.

"Founder, please let go of my brother," said Kiriah. She looked at him with a pleading expression. "He didn't mean it. Rii's always been bad with words. Sometimes he says stupid things like that. It's not his fault he doesn't know how to word things correctly. He's new, anyway, and he's still learning how to speak respectfully to you."

The Founder looked like he was about to disregard my sister's (admittedly more accurate than I would ever like to admit) words about me and finish me off anyway. Indeed, he looked so serious in his attempt to kill me that I began to pray to the Old Gods for a safe journey to their Abode once mine life had left me.

But then the Founder let go and I fell to the floor. I landed on my back, gasping for the sweet, sweet air that now began to fill my lungs, too weak to sit up. Kiriah was by my side instantly, cradling my head in her lap with a look of concern on her face.

"Rii, how do you feel?" asked Kiriah. "Can you still breathe? Will you be okay?"

I coughed loudly, but managed to say, "Yea … sister. I will

live."

Kiriah's brilliant smile brought me more comfort than anything else. Then she looked up at the Founder, and I did also, for I was anxious to see his expression.

For the first time since I had known the Founder, he looked upon us both with cold disdain. I had always thought of the Founder as a much kinder man, but now I saw his robotic half much more clearly than his human half. His cold gaze reminded me of the images of the Old Gods that I had seen in the Divine Books, which depicted the deities with serious, stern expressions that allowed little room for humor and kindness.

And for once, I 'twas indeed afraid of the Founder, as afraid of him as I was of Falnoth the Faceless.

"Both of you must leave now," said the Founder. All of the warmth in his voice had truly drained away. "Force the workers to work harder than they have ever worked in their whole lives. Tell the Delanians to work even harder than that. Allow no one to rest. The Mission *must* be completed, and if anyone objects, I give you full permission to kill them as an example to the others, Kiriah."

Mine sister nodded, though 'twas a shaky nod that I doubted was sincere. "Yes, Founder, I will."

"Good," said the Founder. "I will now retire to my chambers. When the Unification Stones are fully uncovered, then I will initiate the final stages of the Mission. And the worlds will finally be healed."

With that, the Founder turned and walked back into his room. He then slammed the door shut behind him, leaving Kiriah and I on the floor together, staring at the door.

Chapter Eight

Because I was so wounded by the Founder's choke on me, Kiriah sent me to the medical room. She told me, with that same sisterly concern that I so loved about her, that I needed to rest and heal, that Reunification would be fine without me for a little while, and that I need not overexert mine self in my current state.

For once, I didst not argue with Kiriah. I saw that she was correct, for mine throat hurt so badly that even breathing was difficult, to say the least. It would heal—of that I had no doubt—but in order for it to heal, I would need to rest.

'Twas a few minutes later, then, that I found myself lying on a bed in a familiar square room with a view of the pit and construction workers outside. I saw the large cranes already in movement, swinging across the pit, and heard the shouts of the workers. I didst also hear the sounds of the drills and diggers roaring to life, but that hardly filled me with hope, for I questioned whether the workers would be able to work fast enough to dig up the Unification Stone in its entirety before the J bots arrived.

In any case, I was not alone. Lying on the bed next to me was

Sura, who no longer had the bandages covering his face; indeed, his face looked better than ever, his skin clear and his jaw in one piece. It must have been the work of the medical machines of Reunification, which surprised me not, for it had been those same machines which had healed me and done a fine job of it, aside from the aches in the back of mine head every now and then.

Sura was even awake, although he had not said a word to me yet. His eyes were focused on the work outside, which he watched with interest, though I knew not what he found so interesting about it. He did not even seem to be as disturbed as the rest of us, though mayhaps that had to do with the fact that he was not a member of Reunification like the rest of us and therefore had far less at stake in the event of our losing to the J bots than Kiriah or I did.

Then he looked at me and said, "Brother, what happened to your neck? It looks as though one of those infernal robots tried to choke ye."

Rubbing mine neck, I felt the imprints of the Founder's mechanical fingers impressed deeply into mine skin. I knew not how it looked, but I imagined it must have appeared awful indeed.

I could have said that the Founder had done it, that the Founder had tried to murder me for the simple fact that I doubted the wisdom of his current leadership, but I hesitated. Hanging from the ceiling in one corner of the room 'twas one of our security cameras. This machine did observe us at all times, and likely recorded every word we said. If the security operator on the other side of the camera (though I knew not who it 'twas, for I had never met the man and no one had ever told me his name) heard me complaining about the Founder, then he might rethink his decision to spare me.

Therefore, I said to Sura, in a voice still weak from the choking, "'Twas nothing, brother, but an accident. Ye need not worry about my health; instead, worry about your own, although I see that ye are recovering swiftly already."

"Yea, brother, I am," said Sura, nodding. He looked up at the ceiling. "Thanks be to the Old Gods, for they have answered mine prayers of a swift and speedy recovery. Though I will admit, I would much rather be at home than here."

"I understand, brother, but our childhood home is hardly a safe place to be right now," I said.

"Could not the same be said of this place?" said Sura. He gestured toward the window. "I know not exactly what has caused the tension which hangs over this place like a rain cloud, but I have heard whispers of a danger coming to this place. I suspect that this building will soon be no safer than any other part of the world."

"Of that, ye are probably correct," I said with a sigh. "But I do not believe I can tell ye much, for Reunification has a strict policy of keeping outsiders in the dark about the goings-on in our bases. Suffice to say that it is a rather ugly turn of events."

"That is fine, brother," said Sura, leaning back against his fluffy white pillow. "'Tis not an issue to me. I have been treated quite well by your allies, though I will admit that the two agents who brought me here—Arn and Lauz, I believe their names were—did bump my head against the frame of the door when they were bringing me in here."

Sura nodded at the door on the other side of the room, which did make me groan, for I had given those two explicit instructions to carry Sura into this room carefully. Granted, Sura looked fine to me, but I was still determined to speak sternly with Arn and Lauz later, perhaps after the Mission was complete (assuming, of course, we were not all arrested by the J bots and taken away from here).

Rubbing the spot on his head where he was likely bumped, Sura said, "Aside from that, however, I am fine. I have not yet seen Kiriah, however. How is our sister?"

"She is busy," I said. I glanced at the camera watching us from the ceiling. "As the Leader of Reunification, she has many jobs and duties, especially with this recent turn of events. I know not when she will be able to see ye."

Sura's shoulders slumped. "I see. 'Twas hoping to see her soon, but I see that our reunion will have to be pushed back a little. That is fine, I suppose, as neither of us are going anywhere."

I wanted to say that I was not so certain of that, but I kept mine mouth shut. The Old Gods were always listening to us, after all, even in their prison on the moon. Often they took great delight in making our worst fears come true; 'twas why I so rarely tempted fate.

So I decided to change the subject. I wished to ask Sura more about those shadow hands, even though he clearly knew as much about them as I did, but for some reason I found mine self hesitating. I knew not why until I looked at the security camera again and realized that I was hesitating because I did not wish for whoever controlled that camera to learn about Sura's powers.

That made no sense, however. After all, I could trust Reunification, could I not? If they knew of Sura's mysterious powers, so what? They might even be able to aid us in understanding how Sura attained this strange magic. The Founder, having nearly infinite knowledge and wisdom, would likely know just what the cause was or at least would be able to point us in the right direction so we could discover its source ourselves.

But then I remembered Resita and his torture scars; and I remembered the Founder and his mechanical fingers tightening 'round mine windpipe, choking me to death. These memories did make me hesitate, for they revealed another side of Reunification, one I had not been aware of until just recently, but which I thought must have been there all along, like bugs stuck to the underside of a rock.

I doubted they would torture Sura … but then, what if they deemed him a threat to Reunification's operations? I remembered well how Sura's shadow hands killed all twelve of those villains earlier in less time than it took to step through a Portal betwixt Dela and Xeeo. With that kind of power, he could easily destroy Reunification from within.

Of course, Sura did not seem likely to do that, for all he wanted to do was see Kiriah again. Still, the Founder might disagree. He might have the others take Sura and lock him away deep inside the dungeons, where he could not escape. He may even try to kill him, for I had seen insanity in the Founder's eyes earlier and a willingness to do whatever he thought necessary to ensure the completion of the Mission.

'Twould not be right of me to reveal Sura's secrets like this. I would need to somehow guarantee our privacy, though I knew not how to do that, for I could not deactivate the camera from this room. I would need access to the security center, where all of the security cameras connected to, but I could not access that room very easily at the moment, either.

Hence, I decided to rest, seeing as it was all I could do for now. Although I wondered if I even would be able to rest in this situation; the tension 'twas so palpable that I felt it even with only calm Sura in the room near me.

I was about to close mine eyes when Sura said, "Brother, there is something I wish to speak with ye about."

I looked at Sura, who was now looking at me. His hands were folded over his lap, but I could tell he was not going to be sleeping anytime soon.

"Yea, brother?" I said. "What do ye wish to speak about?"

"A dream I had," said Sura, gesturing at his head. "And not one long ago, but a recent one, when I was still unconscious. I wish to speak with ye about it because it did worry me, although I do not understand entirely what it means."

Seeing as I had nothing better to do, I nodded. "Of course, brother. Speak, and I shall listen."

"Very well," said Sura. "In mine dream, I stood on the moon of Dela, near the great pit where the Old Gods were said to have been banished years ago. The dream was so real that at first I thought not it was a dream at all, but a true event."

"Dreams are sometimes like that," I said. "But continue. I am listening."

Sura looked troubled, but he did continue to speak. "In my dream, I leaned over the lip of the maw, for I hoped to see the Old Gods down there. Again, I still did not entirely accept this as a dream, for this dream did seem so real; hence why I looked. But do you know what I saw instead?"

I shook mine head. "Nay, brother, I do not."

"Instead of the Old Gods, I saw things crawling up the walls of the maw," said Sura. "They looked like the tentacles of a monster, reaching up from the depths of the ocean to grasp whatever was within their reach. This did make me back away, but before I could get away from its grasp, one of the tentacles grabbed me and pulled me into the dark maw."

"How terrifying," I said. "What happened after that?"

"I was drawn into a deep world of sheer darkness," said Sura. "'Twas like that one dream I had years ago, when Kiriah first vanished. Only this time, it felt more real than ever. I thought for certain that I was going to die. In the darkness, I heard and felt many different things, but the only thing I remember from that dream is a rather quaint image I can make neither heads nor tales of."

"And what might that image be?" I asked.

"'Twas the image of a little blonde girl and a robot friend of the same size," said Sura. He rubbed his forehead; much to my alarm, he was sweating. "There was a little boy with them, too, a boy with similar blonde hair to the girl, so I assumed they were siblings of a sort. The two siblings and the robot stood together, arm in arm, smiling at me, but I knew not what they were smiling about."

"How queer," I said. "Did ye recognize the two little children at all?"

"Nay, for I have never seen them before," said Sura, shaking his head. "The little girl did remind me of Kiriah when she was that age, but strangely the girl had tiny white bird wings on her back. And they were real wings, too, not some sort of artificial wings strapped onto her or anything of that kind."

"Was that a vision from the Old Gods?" I asked. "It certainly sounds like one to me."

"I believe so," said Sura. "The Divine Books do indeed say that the Old Gods send visions to their priests. Even so, I barely understood this vision; in fact, I do not understand it at all, hence why I am sharing it with ye, for I thought ye might be able to help me understand it."

"It is as opaque to me as it is to ye, brother," I said with a shrug. "It could mean anything. I am no dream-reader; therefore, I can be of no help to ye, as much as I wish I could be."

"Yea, I thought ye might say something like that," said Sura with a sigh. "That is an issue, for I feel that this vision is of great importance. If I had the Divine Books with me, then maybe I would be able to discover the dream's meaning within the pages of those books."

"We will retrieve the Divine Books at some point," I said. "Not today; nay, unlikely anytime soon. But we will. I promise ye that."

"Thank ye for your promise, brother," said Sura, nodding. "It is quite kind. I am certain that the Old Gods appreciate it as well."

"I hope they do, brother," I said. "I hope they do."

Sometime later, I awoke without even realizing that I had drifted off to sleep. How I had managed to sleep with the racket of the construction workers and equipment out there, I knew not, but the fact that I felt so well-rested and breathing was no longer painful was proof enough that I had indeed slept, and well. A quick glance to mine left showed that Sura, too, slept, and much more deeply than I.

As for why I awoke, I did not know until I heard Assassin's familiar voice say, "Get up, Apakerec. You're needed."

I looked up. Assassin's featureless face plate was aimed down at me. Although it may have had no features, I had little trouble telling how disgusted that this machine was with me. No doubt he did not enjoy having to speak with me, and the feeling was mutual, although I was too curious to find out why he was here than to tell him how I felt about him.

At his side was his long, deadly-looking sword. Every time I looked at it, I had to suppress a shudder. I found myself imagining how it would feel for something so large and sharp to stab into me; indeed, every time I did, mine stomach did ache sharply. I always thought that that was due to my imagination, for Assassin, despite his obvious dislike of me, had never stabbed me with his blade (for which I was quite thankful).

"Did ye just tell me to get up?" I said, rubbing the sleep out of mine eyes as I did so. "May I ask why?"

"Because the Leader said we need every able-bodied agent to defend the base from the J bots that are coming," said Assassin. "That includes you, by the way, even though you are quite out of shape."

That little jab of his did annoy me, but I said instead, "Of course I will help to defend the base. But what about the automated defense systems? Do we not have any?"

"We have none," said Assassin. "We've never had to worry about a large-scale attack from anyone, not even from the Foundation. That essentially makes it our job to protect the base."

I raised an eyebrow. "*Our* job? Are ye going to be helping

me?"

"Yes," said Assassin, nodding. "As a robot myself, I will have an easier time fighting the J bots than you organics. I know all of their strategies and tactics, but they don't know any of mine, which will make this quite an interesting battle."

"All right," I said as I threw the covers off of the lower half of mine body and swung my legs over the side of mine bed. "I shall come with ye speedily."

We exited the room, leaving Sura—who had not stirred at all in his sleep—behind to rest. We emerged into one of the long, empty hallways of the headquarters and began walking down the hall toward the teleporter at the end. Even from in here, I could still hear the cacophonous noise of the drills and cranes outside, though it was somewhat muted thanks to the thicker walls betwixt here and the outside.

As we walked, I glanced at Assassin. The robot was clearly not interested in talking to me anymore than he absolutely had to, but I recalled how he had come down to the dungeons to silence Resita. I was tempted to ask him how Resita was doing, but I also feared that he might simply brush off mine questions. After all, perhaps everyone was right, that this Resita person deserved whatever we were doing to him and that it was none of mine business to question it, at least openly and where the Founder could hear me, anyway.

Even so, I could not help but remember how pitiful Resita had looked, how he had insisted that we had known each other, even been friends. That did leave me confused and unsettled, and I loathed feeling either way. I required closure on this matter and I could only receive that closure from Assassin, even if he did not wish to speak with me about it.

Thus, I said, "Assassin, how is the prisoner, Resita, doing? I have not heard about him ever since I saw him in the dungeons below."

"Sleeping," said Assassin, without looking at me. "I told him to stop messing with the wiring of our headquarters. So he went to sleep, because he has nothing better to do."

That did not sound very convincing to me. Resita did not appear like the kind of person who would merely go to sleep after being treated so horribly by us. He likely wasn't asleep at all, although I doubted he was dead, seeing as Assassin seemed unlikely to me to kill one of our prisoners, at least without orders from Kiriah, the Elders, or the Founder.

Still, I decided to push the subject just a mite, for I was still interested in finding out about him. Did seem like an important matter to me, despite mine certainty that I had never met Resita before this day.

"Have we learned anything of importance from Resita?" I asked. "Since capturing him, I mean."

"Classified," said Assassin, again keeping his face plate forward. "Only the Leader, the Elders, and the Founder are allowed to know that information. Because you're a low-level agent, you are not allowed to know what we have learned, even if you are the older brother of the Leader."

I frowned. "Are ye certain of that?"

Assassin's blade was at mine neck before I even realized it, forcing me to stop to avoid slitting my throat against its wickedly sharp blade. I looked at Assassin, whose featureless face plate was now facing me. Whilst he had no facial expression at all, I could imagine how angry he would have looked if he had one.

"Stop asking stupid questions," said Assassin. "Especially stupid questions that are irrelevant to our current situation. The status of the prisoner is information that is only supposed to be known by our leaders. You were not even supposed to—oh, never mind. Let's just keep going."

Assassin lowered his sword and stomped ahead of me, his metal feet clanging loudly against the tiled floor. I stood there in shock for a few seconds before shaking mine head and hurrying after him. Only this time, I kept behind him and did not ask him any questions. 'Twas, perhaps, not the time to ask him a thing.

Soon we were out in the heat of the Dead Lands, which, despite the dark night, made my forehead break out into a sweat. Mine robes were still heavy, which made me feel warmer than usual. But I did not complain, because I knew that complaining 'twas fruitless, for none of my fellow agents out here—Assassin, Arn, and Lauz—would give me much sympathy or understanding (especially Assassin).

We stood on top of the massive walls of dirt that had been piled up around the rim of the pit. These walls were quite hard and packed together, which made them much sturdier 'neath our feet than ye would think; still, they were quite a ways above the sandy, rocky earth on the other side, which stretched out in the distance for as far as the eye could see, illuminated by the moon and stars above.

The Dead Lands stretched out in every direction for miles. All I saw was sand, boulders and massive rock structures that protruded from the earth, canyons and grottos that were home to only-the-Old-Gods-knew what. There was not a stream of water —nay, not even a trickle—to be seen anywhere, although I knew that there were a few underwater lakes from which Reunification drew water for its headquarters. Nor did I see any animals; whilst I knew that the Dead Lands did have its own wildlife, right now, I saw no sign of any living thing down there. Very few creatures could survive in this hostile and harsh environment; indeed, even many machines would have a difficult time out here, for the heat even at night was strong enough to short-circuit any machines which were not equipped to handle it.

Although perhaps I should not have said that there was *no* life in this place. Down below, at the base of the walls, was our army of Lizard-men, also known as Hunters, moving about and snarling. There were about one hundred in all, which was a goodly amount, although whether they would be of any use against the J bots that were coming, I knew not. Still, Assassin had said that the Lizard-men were capable of dismantling any J bots that came this way; hence, he had said, we should place our trust in them and try to avoid getting in their way.

That may have been so, but as I looked down upon the Lizard-men below, I felt quite glad that they were all down there and not up here with us. Seeing those humanoid, lizard-like abominations —yea, 'twas what I thought of them, due to their origin as children of gene splicers—made the back of mine head hurt and caused my heart to beat with fear. 'Twas as though my body was remembering a negative past experience with them, although since joining Reunification, I had never had to fight these creatures, nor even personally interacted with them.

Shaking mine head, I looked up into the distance. I saw

nothing on the horizon, nothing save rock spires and tall hills rising. The moon and stars were high in the sky; even so, the air in the Dead Lands was still uncomfortably hot. I took a swig of ice cold water from my flask, which Arn had been kind enough to give to me when Assassin and I had arrived. 'Twas the most brilliant and beautiful water I had ever drank; indeed, it was almost like the nectar of the Old Gods in this heat.

Behind us was the loud noises of the drills burrowing into the earth, workers shouting and yelling instructions or requests back to each other, and the creaking of the cranes as they lifted or moved things about in the pit. It sounded to me like the workers were working faster than ever, which was a goodly thing, for the Unification Stone was not going to dig up itself. I also wondered if our brothers on Dela were doing the same thing, though I supposed that there was no way to know that for certain.

"Assassin, do ye know how much longer until our enemies arrive?" I asked, looking at the robot, who stood so still that he appeared to be almost entirely nonfunctional.

"No," said Assassin, shaking his head. "We don't even know if the J bots have left their headquarters yet. My guess is that they already have—those J bots typically do not delay following an anonymous tip, especially one that gives them sensitive information, like the coordinates of our base—but again, I don't know."

"We will be able to beat them back anyway," I said. "Right?"

"Of course," Arn broke in. Unlike Assassin and me, he carried a large bazooka of some sort, which he claimed to know how to use, although its size and power did worry me greatly. "We will fight to the death for the Mission. That is what we're all here for, right, Lauz?"

Lauz nodded. Unlike the rest of us, Lauz's hands were free; however, he wore a vest with twin laser guns rising from the shoulders, which appeared operated by a keypad on the chest. 'Twas the oddest Xeeonite weapon I had ever seen, but in some ways, it was the most brilliant, for it left his hands open for anything else he needed to do. Of course, I would never be caught dead wearing it, for despite its efficiency, I thought it looked quite silly.

Again, I looked to the horizon, squinting mine eyes to see if I could spot our enemies before they could see us. I still saw nothing against the bluish white horizon, which made me wonder whether they would even be coming at all. Despite Assassin's assurances that the J bots always followed up on anonymous tips, I wondered whether any of them would actually come out this far to investigate. We were quite a ways away from Xeeon, or any other Xeeonite city for that matter. It might take them days or even weeks to reach this place, by which time the Mission might very well be completed.

As I thought that, Assassin pointed into the distance. "Incoming enemy cruiser."

I looked into the distance again. At first, I still did not see anything; but 'twas only a few seconds later that a small black dot had appeared on the horizon, which flew over the rock spies and sandy dunes below. It was too far away for me to make out in any great detail, but I doubted it was a friendly ship.

"Did ye say cruiser?" I said, looking at Assassin. "What do ye mean by that?"

"A J bot cruiser," Assassin answered. "Also known as a

Lawful Ship. To put it in terms your Delanian mind can grasp, think of a large, metal flying ship carrying Portals for J bots to use to travel to here. And I mean dozens and dozens of Portals, enough that they could unload the entire J bot police force on us if they wanted to."

"A flying ship?" I repeated. "Assassin, I know that ye Xeeonites have created flying vehicles, but I find that difficult to believe. Especially a full-sized, metal flying ship; why, such a machine would be too heavy to stay afloat even one inch above the earth's surface."

"It's the truth," said Assassin. "But if you don't believe me, you will once the ship arrives and dumps a small army of J bots on us."

"Yeah," Arn added. He was staring at the incoming ship, almost trembling in fear. "I've seen those things before. They aren't used often, but those damn ships are a big headache. Think the last time they used them was when the Destroyer got a little too close to Xeeon and they wanted to scare it off, but that was a year ago."

I frowned, still watching the ship drawing ever closer. "Then I suppose we must prepare for the inevitable conflict that will begin as soon as it gets within range."

"Of course," said Assassin. He held his sword in a defensive position. "Kill every J bot you see and that is not smart enough to stay out of the reach of your sword."

I nodded and drew mine skyras sword from my sheath. Pressing the tab, the energy blade materialized immediately, its glowing form slightly radiating heat, although 'twas not as hot as the heat of the Dead Lands itself.

As the flying ship drew ever closer, I thought it looked not like any ship I had ever seen. I saw no sails or steering wheel, nor a port or a bow. It more closely resembled a flying disk, a saucer of some sort, with a black paint job that looked deadly even from a distance. It seemed odd to me to call it a 'ship,' but then again, perhaps the Xeeonites had a different definition of that word than we Delanians did.

The ship resembled a flying disk of death, rotating wildly through the air as it flew ever closer to us. Red and green lights shone from its sides, but it had no windows that I could see, nothing to allow me or the others to peer inside and find out who was piloting it.

In addition, it 'twas extremely loud, so loud that it drowned out the noises of the construction work behind us and the frightened and angry cries of the Lizard-men below. 'Twas likely the ship's engine, which was almost as loud as a bomb.

But still, I held mine ground, looking up at it as it closed the distance betwixt itself and the pit with every passing second. So did my allies, though 'twas hard to tell what Assassin was feeling, for Assassin's face plate and body language were impossible to read. As for the other two, Arn raised his massive bazooka, whilst Lauz took up a fighting stance, aiming both of his shoulder-mounted lasers at the incoming ship.

All of us waited and waited, watching the disk come ever closer, with no sign that it was slowing down. We waited every minute, not daring to speak or do much of anything, for our concentration was wholly on the incoming enemy ship, which flew toward us like a winged beast seeking to eliminate us.

And then it began to drop small, disk-shaped machines from

its underside, dozens and dozens of them in fact. The machines did not fall to the ground, however; instead, they flew through the air toward us, carried along by booster rockets I could not hear due to the noisiness of the infernal disk itself.

It was not long before I recognized the disks for what they were: Portals, flying Portals, which soared through the air toward us, just as Assassin described. They came at a frightening speed, coming so fast that I was almost afraid of them, even though the Portals were unarmed.

Then the Portals stopped in midair and righted themselves. They floated dozens of feet away from us, too far for us to hit them (at least, Assassin and I could not, but Arn and Lauz might have been able to, thanks to their long-range weapons). The Portals hovered in the air for a brief moment before they activated, causing vortexes to appear within them like blazing flames.

And from within that fire came J bot after J bot, carrying their rifles before them like soldiers going to war, flying straight toward us at a terrifying speed. The army of metallic warriors came at us so fast that I feared we would be overrun, that all our efforts would be for naught.

But then, with a foul yell, Arn fired a massive missile at the incoming army. Many of them swerved out of the way of the missile, but a handful that were too slow received a direct hit, causing them to explode into a fiery mess that fell down onto the scrambling Lizard-men below, which were now climbing the wall in order to join us up here.

Lauz then fired his own lasers at the J bots, but again, most of them dodged, although he did hit one out of the air, causing it to smash into the wall upon which we stood and explode.

As for Assassin, he raised hand and unleashed electricity at the J bots. He succeeded in striking a few out of the air, though the others managed to avoid it. Still, 'twas satisfying to see those few he had hit fall to the earth below, where the Lizard-men awaited their opportunity to tear them apart,

I paid no attention to that, however, because I now swung my skyras sword every which way in an attempt to hit the invaders. Yet mine sword did not touch them, for they flew over over and out of mine reach, which made me wish that I had brought a projectile weapon with me. All I could do was watch the J bots we did not hit fly over me into the main area of the pit, but I could not stop them, for more J bots kept emerging from the Portals.

Even worse, the J bots were firing their own energy bolts at us from their rifles. The energy bolts forced the four of us to scatter and separate, attempting to avoid being struck down by the sizzling bolts that struck the ground all around us.

Then two of the J bots landed on either side of me, cutting me off from mine fellow Reunification agents. They aimed their guns at me, but I did not give them a chance to fire. I spun around, holding mine skyras sword out, striking the tips of their guns and rendering them useless.

Yet that did little to stop the two J bots who had surrounded me. As if they had trained for this moment, they tossed their guns aside and advanced on me with electricity sparking betwixt their fingers. Their cold, emotionless gaze made them seem even more threatening, but I did not allow fear to conquer me, for fear would be a burden rather than an aid in this situation.

Yelling, I slashed at the nearest J bot, striking it in the chest, although mine blow only seemed to graze its metallic skin. Its brother reached for me, but I spun around and cut off its hand, revealing its wiring that sparked just as another six or so J bots soared by overhead.

Unfortunately, the J bot simply pointed its other hand at me and fired lightning bolts that reminded me of Assassin's attack. I deflected the lightning bolts with mine sword, but they struck me so hard that I staggered backward.

That J bot's friend took notice of mine opening, for it raised its hands and fired more lightning bolts at me. 'Twas no way I could deflect the bolts in time, for I was still off-guard from its ally's earlier attack.

But then Assassin appeared betwixt me and the bolts and deflected them with his sword. The lightning bolts flew into the sky, nearly striking some of the J bots that were flying overhead.

Then Assassin dashed forward and beheaded the J bot that had attempted to kill me. He then kicked its body backward off the side of the wall, where it vanished from mine sight.

The J bot's hand-less ally aimed its remaining hand at Assassin, but mine robotic ally was upon it in a nanosecond. He stabbed it in the chest with his sword, causing more electricity to spark from it, and then tore out his sword and cut its head clean off, causing its body to collapse at his feet.

But I had no time in which to thank Assassin for coming to mine aid, for the J bot army was still coming fast and furious. Arn and Lauz still fired their weapons at the invaders, but they succeeded only in hitting a very few. Most of the J bots barely took any interest in us; instead, they flew into the pit area, where they flew around firing stunning energy bolts at the workers or landing on our construction equipment and disabling it. About a dozen had landed on or near the headquarters itself, bashing in windows or shooting holes in the ceiling in order to enter. A few even went straight down into the pit itself, which to me was as good a sign as any that our entire Mission was doomed.

Even so, I did not give up. Despite mine earlier doubts about Reunification, I was determined to keep going no matter how grim our current situation appeared.

But I knew not how to help, for there were too many J bots for me to battle and I had no projectile weapon to use to shoot them with. It did seem that all I could do was stand here and watch as the Mission fell apart all around me.

Shaking mine head to snap myself out of those depressing thoughts, I turned and ran to the edge of the wall I stood upon. Looking down, I saw the Lizard-men still scaling the wall, but they were a disorganized mess—constantly pulling each other down in their quest to be the first up here—that I knew we could not rely on them to save us.

Therefore, I looked up at the Portals and the ship ahead of me. Did seem like our only chance was to shut off the Portals, but I knew not how to do that, for the Portals were too far away for me to hit. Besides, the ship likely carried many more, which meant that even if we succeeded in destroying those foul Portals, the disk-shaped ship would simply send out more.

Thus, I had to figure out a way to destroy the ship. Yet how could I destroy it if I was nowhere near it? Indeed, it did seem like a hopeless thing to me, this situation did. There were now so many J bots that I could hardly count them, with more emerging from the Portals every minute.

I looked at mine allies standing on the wall with me. Assassin was dueling with three J bots that had landed around him, whilst Arn and Lauz were still firing off shot after shot at the flying enemies. Their aim was quite poor, however, for they missed many and hit only a few. I wanted to scream at them to aim for the Portals, but I doubted they could hear me in this chaos.

Instead, I seized one of the energy rifles that one of the J bots must have dropped at some point off of the ground and took aim at the nearest Portal (although I first had to put away mine skyras sword to do so). Mine aim was not much good, due to my lack of experience using these types of weapons, but I understood the basics of how these guns worked and was determined to use it even if I was no master marksman.

Aiming for one of the Portals' boosters, I pulled the trigger on the rifle, sending an energy bolt flying from its tip. The blow back, however, sent me staggering backwards, for I was unused to firing guns; even so, I found that I had enjoyed the sensation of the blast anyway.

I only dwelt on that feeling for but a moment, however, for I saw the energy bolt hurtling through the air toward the Portal's right booster. Like Zaunas's lightning, the energy bolt struck the booster dead on.

When the energy bolt struck, the booster exploded, setting the bottom right corner of the Portal aflame, but rather than fall straight down, the Portal careened to the left. It struck the Portal right next to it, knocking out one of its boosters and sending both of them falling to the ground below, where they crashed with such an almighty explosion that it sent a fireball flying into the air.

That did fill me with a sense of satisfaction, but just as those

Portals exploded, two more fell from the ship's open hold and flew back to replace their fallen brothers immediately. Even though I had expected something like that to happen, it still caused mine heart to drop into a deep depression, for now I was all but certain that the Mission was indeed a failure and that Reunification was not blessed by the Old Gods.

Hence, I threw the rifle to the ground and fell to my hands and knees, staring up at the J bots that kept coming. Nearby, Arn had somehow lost his bazooka and was pinned to the top of the wall by three J bots, while the laser cannons on Lauz's shoulders hung limply, as if broken, around his body as he attempted to wrestle with a J bot, although I could tell that he was not going to win that particular fight.

I glanced over mine shoulder and saw Assassin now surrounded by a dozen J bots. He fought them ferociously, using both his sword and his electricity, but the J bots kept coming and it 'twas quite clear to me that it was only a matter of time before they overwhelmed him with sheer numbers.

Oddly, despite the feelings of defeat rising in mine soul, a part of me felt satisfied that Reunification was coming to its end. After all, had I not seen the darker side of this organization? Perhaps it would be better for us all if Reunification fell and the Mission was left incomplete.

Just as I thought that, however, I spotted movement in the shadow of the giant disk ship. Ignoring the sounds and scenes of battle all around me, I looked at the gigantic shadow 'neath the ship. I at first saw nothing within its shadow save for sand and rock, but then a huge, shadowy hand rose from the darkness toward the machine itself.

ALLEGIANCE

I watched in shock and curiosity as the massive hand seized the underside of the ship like the Old Gods seizing the sun. Then it pulled the massive ship down to the ground faster than I thought something of that size ought to have been able to do. The ship did not even fight against the hand, likely because its pilot had been taken by surprise.

When the ship smashed into the earth, it created a massive explosion which rent mine ears and forced me to duck and cover. Flaming hot debris flew over me, just barely missing mine head, while the startled screams and roars of the Lizard-men rose from below like wind blowing from a tunnel. The explosion briefly lit the night, but it was only for a moment before the light died away.

Then I looked up and saw that many of the J bots were now flying toward the massive, disk-shaped wreck on the ground below, likely to go find out what had happened—only, that turned out to be a foolish move, for shadow hands shot out from the shadows of some nearby boulders and seized the J bots and dragged them into the darkness before they could so much as shout.

The J bots which had been attacking Arn and Lauz had been among the robots that had been flying over to see what had caused the crash. Lauz was helping Arn up, but was hardly looking down at his best friend, for he was now staring at the wreckage of the massive ship below, which continued to burn under the moon of the Dead Lands, whilst the Lizard-men were now hopping and running around it. The Lizard-men seemed to be trying to understand what had happened; indeed, so was I, although I had a better inkling of what had occurred than they, in their tiny lizard brains, did.

Assassin dashed up to mine side. He, too, was looking down at the massive fallen ship below and even seemed surprised, although again his expressionless face plate made that impossible to tell for certain. All I could tell for sure was that Assassin's body was covered in black burn marks and dented in several places, no doubt caused by the J bots he had been fighting moments ago.

"What happened?" said Assassin. He turned his face plate toward me. "What was that? Did you somehow knock that ship out of the sky?"

Before I could answer, the loud sound of dozens of energy blasts being fired at once made me stand up and run back to the other side of the wall, where I would get a better look of the pit. Assassin, Arn, and Lauz joined me and the four of us stood together watching the strange event playing out below.

Whilst there were still many J bots flying around, their numbers were rapidly dwindling before mine eyes. Shadow hands —much smaller than the huge one that had downed the ship, although in no way any less dangerous—shot out from the darkness of the pit and snatched at every J bot that flew too close. The sudden appearance of the shadow hands appeared to have taken most of those villains by surprise, for many were snatched and dragged into the shadows without so much as a word.

But some did indeed have enough to sense to attempt to fight back. They fired their energy rifles at the shadow hands, but their energy bolts merely passed through the shadow hands like they were nothing. Some of the bots fired lightning from their fingers, but again, the shadow hands were completely unaffected. Like an incoming storm, the shadow hands could not be stopped. They came one after another; in fact, a particularly quick J bot was caught betwixt two hands and then ripped in half, creating a sound which was music to mine ears.

"Rii!" a voice shouted to mine left, causing mine head to whip in that direction.

'Twas mine brother Sura, running toward me, his white robes flowing behind him and reflecting the bright rays of the sun above. He did look as strong as ever now, which did make me glad, for I had worried about his health during this battle. But then I noticed the black lines crawling up his neck, though he hid them by pulling up the collar of his robes as he approached me.

"Brother!" I said, spreading my arms as he skid to a stop a few feet from me. "How did ye find me up here? Furthermore, how did ye even get out of our headquarters?"

Panting, Sura wiped the sweat from his brow and said, "Well, brother, I heard ye and your robot friend here discussing where ye would go. The layout of Reunification's headquarters 'twas slightly hard for me to figure out—hence why I took so long to arrive—but after a little trial-and-error, I did indeed find my way here."

"What are you doing out here?" said Assassin, looking at mine brother. He pointed with his sword at the main building. "You should be down in there. Not out here."

"That is an odd thanks I get for saving ye," said Sura, gesturing at the shadow hands continuing to grab at the J bots below. "Did Rii not tell ye of mine power?"

"Wait a minute," said Lauz, who tore his attention away from the scene below to look at mine older brother. "Those scary shadow hands are *yours*?"

"Indeed," said Sura, nodding. "They are under mine complete

control. Hence why they have not attacked any of ye members of Reunification; whilst I am no member myself, I trust mine brother and mine sister's good judgment of ye and I decided to help the only way I knew how."

"Brother, ye are wonderful," I said. "I know that the Old Gods are likely smiling down upon ye now. Truly, ye are their priest."

Sura shrugged. "Well, brother, ye are family and family is—"

He was interrupted by the sudden loud sound of a J bot's boosters, which sounded like a ghost dragon bellowing flame upon us. I looked up in time to see a J bot flying toward us as quickly as lightning, zigzagging through the air to avoid the shadow hands trying to stop it.

The J bot then landed on its feet right behind Sura. Without hesitation, the J bot seized Sura's right arm and twisted it behind his back, causing Sura to cry out in pain before the J bot—which had red accents on its metallic armor—wrapped its fingers around Sura's neck.

I immediately drew mine skyras sword again and activated its blade, whilst Assassin held up his sword, but then the J bot said, "Drop your weapons or I will kill your ally."

The J bot spoke with such coldness that I had no doubt in mine heart of hearts that it would indeed kill Sura if we tried to save him. That did seem out-of-character for the J bots, who as I understood it always attempted to bring in criminals alive, but then, perhaps these J bots were more willing to perform drastic measures in order to defeat us than they usually were.

"Let mine brother go," I said, waving mine sword before me. "Or else."

"Negative," said the J bot, shaking its head. "Sensors indicate that this human is the source of the unexplained phenomena that is destroying my fellow officers. He radiates an unusual amount of skyras; therefore, if I kill or disable him, then the phenomena will cease and it will still be possible to salvage the mission. I will only spare his life if you surrender."

Sura said not a word, but he did look at me with terrified eyes. He clearly wanted us to save him, but I knew not how, for if any of us tried anything, then the J bot would simply take his life. This machine had no conscience, for robots were incapable of knowing of such higher things as morality and righteousness, which meant that it could not be reasoned with in a philosophical debate of any sort. Even Assassin, easily the fastest and most brutal of us, would be unlikely to slay the J bot before he forced mine brother to give up the ghost.

Yet I did not wish to drop mine weapons. Whilst the J bots' numbers had been decimated by the shadow hands, there were still far too many for us to fight. To give up now would be to allow them to arrest us; and if they arrested us and threw us behind bars, then the Mission would truly be lost even if our Delanian brothers succeeded in mining their Unification Stone out of the earth in that world.

"I will give you five minutes in which to make your ultimate decision," said the J bot. "Four minutes and fifty-nine seconds remain."

I bit mine lower lip. I tried to see a way out of this, but this seemed like an impossible situation to me. Even Assassin did not seem to have any answer, and I most certainly could not count on either Arn or Lauz to figure out a third option, for the two of them together held as much intelligence and cleverness as a baby deer.

"Four minutes and forty-five seconds," said the J bot. "Four minutes and forty-four—"

The J bot was abruptly interrupted when Kiriah appeared behind it and, in one smooth motion, stabbed it in the back of the head with an energy knife. Electricity sparked from the J bot's head, but Kiriah only dug her knife deeper and deeper into its head. The machine lost its grip on Sura, allowing mine brother to step forward, but rather than run away, he turned around and thrust his hand toward it.

A shadow hand leaped out of the pit below and seized the robot quickly. Then the hand dragged the vile machine straight into the pit, where none of us would ever see it again.

With that villain now gone, Sura thrust his hands toward the rest of the machines flying around the place. What appeared to be a hundred shadow hands—possibly more, but they were so closely bunched together that I could not count them even if I tried—soared out of the pit and seized the remaining J bots. Those few J bots that were not take by surprise tried to fight back, but their efforts were useless, for the hands dragged the machines back into the shadows of the pit, where they vanished into thin air.

The pit was now as silent as the grave. One of the cranes had had its arm swinging from its body by a mere thread, whilst the main building looked like a bomb had gone off in it, based on the broken windows and holes in the roof that I saw. Many of the workers lay paralyzed on the earth, but as far as I could tell, we lost not a single life in this conflict. The stink of smoke and fire did fill mine nostrils, however, and the heat from the burning Ship below did make the night hotter; still, that was bearable, knowing that our victory was complete.

'Twas a miracle of the Old Gods, for certain, which made me pray a quick prayer of gratitude to them for their aid. For how else could ye explain this, if it were not for the grace of the Old Gods blessing us?

Then Kiriah walked up to us. She did not look like she had fought much herself, for her robes were mostly spotless and her hair was in good condition. Yet her eyes, once so wide and innocent, were now narrow and full of caution and anger, despite our overwhelming victory against the enemy. She still carried the energy blade in her hand, though her hand appeared slightly bloodied, no doubt due to the sharp metal pieces which had cut into her skin after she stabbed that robot in the back of his evil head.

"Sister," I said, turning to face her. "Thank ye for rescuing our brother. I did not expect ye to help."

Kiriah brushed some strands of her beautiful blonde hair out of her eyes and said, "And I didn't expect to, either, but when I saw what that awful machine threatened to do to him, I … I snapped."

At that moment, Sura walked up to us as well. His eyes were on Kiriah, looking up and down her form as if he could hardly believe what he was seeing. I had felt much the same way when I had first seen Kiriah two and a half weeks ago; indeed, I still at times had a hard time believing that it was her.

"Kiriah?" said Sura, blinking as he rubbed his right arm, which was no longer twisted. "Is that ye?"

Kiriah turned to face him. She smiled at him now, her beautiful smile that always made me feel better. "Yes, Sura, it's me. It's been a long time, hasn't it?"

Sura opened his mouth to speak, but then Assassin stepped forward and said, "Sorry to interrupt this touching family reunion, Leader, but I would like to know what our next course of action should be, now that the base is safe for the time being."

I did want to punch that stupid machine in the face for daring to interrupt our reunion, for he did not even appear sorry about it. Indeed, I did think that Assassin enjoyed it, for he likely interrupted it in order to annoy me specifically.

Much to my annoyance, Kiriah did not appear as bothered by this needless interruption as I was. She gestured at Assassin and said, "You, Arn, and Lauz can round up the Lizard-men and return them to their cages. Then I want you three to go through the headquarters and make a complete and thorough report on the damages we sustained in the battle, as well as the number of wounded and casualties we suffered. Report back to me in an hour."

"Very well," said Assassin, bowing at mine sister. "Your will is my command, Leader."

Whilst Assassin sounded sincere, I thought he seemed to be mocking mine sister. Granted, he seemed to lack the animosity toward mine sister that he had toward me, but I still thought he 'twas pushing the respectfulness and was about to say so before he stood up and ran off in the other direction. Arn and Lauz followed him and soon only Kiriah, Sura, and I were standing on the wall, illuminated by the flames of the crashed Ship below and the light of the moon and stars above.

"Anyway," said Kiriah, looking at Sura with a smile. "I am so glad that we're all back together again. It's been so long since I last saw your face, brother, that I almost forgot what it looked like."

Sura rubbed his right cheek. "And I, too, nearly forgot your own face, sister. Ye look a little different from how I remember ye, but at the same time, there is no mistaking ye for anyone else."

"This is wonderful," I said, putting mine hand over my heart and causing both of mine siblings to look at me. "We are all together again. That means that we will most assuredly be together once the worlds are reunited and the Mission is complete. This calls for a celebration; a celebration to the Old Gods, whose guiding hand has protected us all up until this point."

"Yea, it does," said Sura, nodding. "Whilst I would love to have the Divine Books on hand so we can properly celebrate, I have memorized most of the relevant—"

"Kiriah, Rii," said another voice behind us, which caused all three of us to turn and see who had spoken it. "I am glad to see that you both survived the assault."

Mine eyes widened when I saw who was walking toward us: 'Twas the Founder himself, striding toward us at an easy, calm pace, as though he were taking a simple stroll down the lane. His hands were placed together like in a prayer, his sleeves covering his hands, and his expression showed not a hint of happiness. Still, I could tell that he was pleased to see that we had survived, a sentiment I shared with him, for our survival indeed gladdened mine own heart as well.

"Founder," said Kiriah. She stood up straight and saluted him. "I ... I did not think you would leave your chambers. What are

Timothy L. Cerepaka

you doing out here?"

The Founder stopped a few feet from us. Despite the heat, he did not appear at all hot in his thick robes. Indeed, he seemed quite at ease, as though content with the way things had turned out.

Even so, I felt more than a mite skittish 'round him, for I remembered how, a little more than an hour ago, he had nearly killed me in his rage. That rage of his—a foul beast if ever I saw one—seemed to be dormant now; perhaps it had simply been the stress of the situation getting to him, a stress that was now relieved thanks to mine brother Sura's heroic efforts.

"I came out here to congratulate you on your victory," said the Founder. He still did not smile, but 'twas easy to hear the approval in his voice. "Even I did not think we would win. I thought we would be crippled and that the worlds would remain separate and in pain. Who is responsible for this victory?"

Kiriah slapped Sura on the shoulder. "My oldest brother, Sura. I don't think you two have met."

The Founder nodded at Sura. "It was you who summoned those shadow hands?"

"Yea," said Sura, nodding. He gestured at the massive, burning wreck of a ship on the other side of the wall below. "'Twas mine doing."

"I find that an interesting power you wield, Sura," said the Founder. "Tell me, how did you come by it?"

Sura shrugged. "I know not how. I had a dream once, years ago, and when I awoke, I could summon the shadows."

Though the Founder's body language had not changed, I somehow sensed an intense fear rise up in him. His expression did

166

change briefly, to a grimace of horror, before it returned to its original plainness.

"There are many unexplained mysteries in the two worlds," said the Founder. "And I suppose you are now one of them. Nonetheless, I must thank you for your help. But not merely thank you; no, I must reward you, as you are deserving of for your efforts."

"Reward?" said Sura. Mine brother perked up at the mention of that word. "What kind of reward? Money? Property? Perhaps fame and power?"

"None of those things," said the Founder. He held out a hand. "Instead, I offer you membership in Reunification. You do not even need to undergo the Ceremony first."

That did surprise me. The Ceremony was something that all new members of Reunification had to go through before they joined. Even I underwent it, though mine memories of the Ceremony were fuzzy owing to the pain in the back of mine head that I felt every time I tried to remember it.

Kiriah and I looked at brother Sura, who was now stroking his chin in thought. Though Sura had turned down mine offer of membership to him already, perhaps he would be more willing to accept the Founder's offer. I saw no reason for him to refuse; after all, he had already rescued us. That made him a member of Reunification as much as anyone, in mine opinion. Besides, he knew too much to simply go home and return to his normal life; he 'twould be a security risk, even if he did not tell anyone what he had learned.

But then, much to my surprise, Sura shook his head. "'Tis very kind of ye to make that offer to me, Founder, but I must decline."

The Founder still held out his hand, but even I could tell that he was displeased by Sura's rejection. "Why?"

"Because I have devoted mine life to the Old Gods, of course," said Sura, gesturing toward the sky above. "Whilst I do not believe that your Mission is totally incompatible with the ways of the Old Gods, I still feel that it would be better for me to stay out of this organization. I do not believe I can fully commit to it as much as mine brother and sister have."

The Founder moved not a muscle on his body. "Are you certain? There is always room for more in the great Mission."

"I am as certain of this decision as I am of every decision I have made," said Sura, "which is to say, quite certain. But I must thank ye for reuniting me with mine sister and brother. I will leave as soon as I am able, for even though I am aware of how unsafe our home is, I know of someone in Xeeo who can keep me hidden from the searching eyes of the Knights of Se-Dela."

"What if I offered you a million delanes?" said the Founder. "I could easily get you that money, and so much more, without having to blink an eye."

"Nay," said Sura, shaking his head. "Mine family is already wealthy beyond measure. I need not more, though if ye did give me the money, perhaps I could donate it to the poor and needy. The cold days are coming, after all, and many of the poor are in desperate need of warming clothing to survive the coming winter."

The Founder stepped forward. His expression still had not changed, but I was beginning to remember how he had treated me earlier, making me fear for whatever he was about to do next.

"But we could use your help," said the Founder. "The Mission is important. More important than anything else in all of the two worlds. You might be able to provide an invaluable service to us with your fantastic powers. Do you not understand that?"

"I understand that ye believe the Mission to be very important," said Sura. "But, and I mean no offense by this, I see it as close to idolatry, your passion for it is. The Old Gods are jealous gods and do not approve of their followers, much less their priests, worshiping false—"

Mine eyes did not follow what happened next; or rather, they followed it as though I were watching a slide show play out before mine eyes.

One moment, the Founder a few feet away from us; the next moment, the Founder was in front of Sura; and in the next, the Founder held Sura by the neck; and in the final moment, the Founder hurled Sura over the side of the wall into the pit below.

I watched, in horror, as Sura fell into the darkness of the pit without so much as a scream. But I could see the look of terror and shock on his features, though it was visible for only a moment; in the next, it was gone, eaten up by the shadows of the pit.

"Sura!" Kiriah and I shouted at the same time. "Brother!"

But there was no answer, save for the echoes of our cries of pain off the walls of the pit. A handful of the workers who were recovering from the J bots' assault looked up, startled by our shouts, but I paid them no attention, for I now rounded on the Founder, almost unable to contain mine rage.

"Founder," I said, mine fingers twitching. "Why did ye do that to Sura? What did Sura ever do to ye?"

The Founder appeared not at all intimidated by mine anger.

He simply met mine angry eyes with his own cold ones, creating a battle of the stares betwixt the two of us.

"You heard your brother's words with your own ears," said the Founder. "He said that he considered the Mission idolatry. We cannot have any doubters or dissenters in Reunification, not when we are so close to the completion of the Mission. And even if we had let him go, he knew too much about us. I had no choice."

I could hardly believe mine ears. The Founder spoke so casually of killing mine brother, as if he had merely stepped on an ant. It angered me so greatly that I could hardly think rationally.

I looked at Kiriah. Her hands were covering her mouth and tears welled in her eyes, yet she seemed unable to speak.

"Kiriah, do ye not agree with me that this is an outrageous act?" I said. "Sura was a good man; more than that, 'twas a good brother. Will ye not join me in condemning the Founder's actions?"

Kiriah looked between me and the Founder several times. She blinked her eyes rapidly, likely in an attempt to stem the flow of tears, but all she succeeded in doing was making her tears flow more freely than ever.

"I … I think …" Kiriah sniffled and gasped. "I think that the Founder … was right. We are so close to completing the Mission now. We can't afford any doubters."

Mine mouth fell open. I had never, not in a million years, ever believed that Kiriah would feel that the murder of our oldest brother was justified. Yet mine own ears, which worked as fine as ever, had indeed told me that mine sister cared more for the Mission than our brother.

"It is no matter," said the Founder, shaking his head. He

walked past me, his robes brushing against my arm as he did so. "Sura is dead, the J bots were crushed, and now all we need to do is unearth the Unification Stone. Soon, the Mission will be—"

I did not let that foul villain finish his sentence. I whirled around, mine skyras sword in hand, and stabbed him directly in the back. The Founder cried out in pain, while Kiriah screamed mine name, but I paid her little attention. I dug mine sword deep into the Founder's back, as hard as I could. He must have been a thick man, for it was very difficult; nonetheless, I did not give up, instead putting more effort into it than ever, asking the Old Gods to give me the strength I needed.

"Rii," the Founder gasped, his voice as weak as death now. "Rii, what are you doing? Cease this nonsense at once."

The back of mine head burned with pain and I wished to obey his commands, but mine desire to avenge Sura overrode whatever brainwashing that the Founder put me through. I listened not to his pleas of mercy.

I thus said, "Nay, Founder. I have seen enough of your evils, of the evils of Reunification, to know that to continue to let ye live would be a great crime against the universe. I will end ye and your talents for evil, end ye right here and now, and the two worlds shall be safe once again."

The Founder did not respond, likely because the life was draining from his body. I saw no blood coming from his wound, but that mattered not, because I did not need to see blood in order to know that he was dying even as I stood there.

That was when I felt a hot energy blade stab deep into the lower part of my back. The pain 'twas so horrible that I cried out in pain and let go of mine skyras sword, which immediately retracted back into the hilt and fell to the ground at mine feet.

I felt the blade in mine back pull out and then turned to see who had stabbed me. Kiriah stood there, a horrified, confused look on her face as she stared at me. The hilt of her energy blade was covered in blood, as was her hand, but I could not comprehend it.

"Sister …" I said, mine voice weak. "Why … why did ye …"

Kiriah did not meet mine eyes, but she said, in a voice much colder than she had ever spoke in before (but which somehow seemed ominously familiar to me), "The Mission must be completed, brother. It *must* be. I am sorry."

Though the pain of her knife hurt me greatly, 'twas the pang of betrayal deep within mine heart that hurt more. I wanted to yell at her for being so foolish, for supporting the Founder over me, but then I felt something heavy slam into the back of mine head. Then the darkness claimed me, and I saw no more.

Coming October 2015:
Two Worlds #4:
Retaliation

Chapter 1

Date: Loday, third day of the week, Gogoth 10th, 3050 XE, 3050 DE

Time: 7:32 PM XST (Xeeon Standard Time), 7:32 AM DST (Delanian Standard Time)

Location: Xeeon, one of the seven city states situated between the Dead Lands and the rest of Xeeo, and the most well-known and populous of them. Population: Three million. Current Mayor is Xacron-Ah, who has reigned over the city for six years. Protected by the J Series Law Enforcement Robots, which were designed and built by Annulus Robotics, Inc.

Objective: Kidnap Mayor Xacron-Ah and take him back to the Foundation's current temporary headquarters for further interrogation.

Status: Power level at 90%.

Timothy L. Cerepaka

I stand on the top of one of Xeeon's massive skyscrapers. The sky is quite dark at the moment, but the city itself is alive with lights. Massive telescreens play ads for products such as the new Intelligent Arm Buddy, as well as news reports from the major Xeeonite news stations and even news from Dela. The streets are full of hundreds of people, who despite the time of night appear as lively and awake as ever.

I do not stand in the open, however. Instead, I stand behind one of the electronic billboards built directly into the skyscraper's roof. I do this because I am trying to avoid the searching optics and sensors of my fellow J bots, who soar through the sky or stand watch on top of other buildings. There aren't many out tonight—they probably do not expect any trouble tonight—but I must remain hidden nonetheless. I wish to join them, but I am aware that returning to my fellow officers would cause more harm than good at the moment, especially if they knew what I am about to do.

As for why they have not sensed me yet, that is because Konoa, one of the Foundation's agents, disabled my connections to the Database and my fellow J bots when he repaired me two and a half weeks ago. I cannot activate the communication channels between me and my fellow J bots or between me and the Database even if I want to.

But it is not merely my own tech preventing me from communicating with my fellow J bots. Leaning against the back of the electronic billboard, her arms crossed over her chest, is the female elf known as Lanresia. On the index finger of her right hand, she wears a black skyras ring that is cloaking us from the sensors of my fellow J bots. I know it works because when she

174

tested it on herself back on Dela, I tried to scan for her presence but failed to find her, even though she had only been standing a few feet away from me at the time.

In contrast to my passive demeanor, Lanresia appears restless and afraid. She constantly rubs her skyras ring, every now and then peeking out from around the billboard to see if she can spot Konoa, although I doubt she can see much with those thick, dark goggles strapped over her eyes. She does not say anything, probably because her speaking snake is deactivated, curled around her waist like a belt, so she cannot speak to me at all.

Not that I am complaining. Our current mission requires as much silence as we are able to create. Speaking is unnecessary; after all, we already spent the past day going over every last detail of the plan. I can recite the entire plan by memory, although I suppose that isn't impressive, seeing as we J bots tend to have picture perfect memory in comparison to organics.

The only reason we have not yet moved from behind the large billboard is because we are awaiting the sign from Konoa. Back on Dela, during the planning stages of this kidnapping, we agreed on a signal for Konoa to give us when it is our turn to move. So far, Konoa has not given us the okay, although I am not disturbed, because we have received no sign so far that Konoa has run into any unexpected problems. He should be giving us the signal any minute now.

As I stand here, I go over the plan in my head, despite having gone over it several times with Lanresia, Konoa, and the Head. Still, we have nothing better to do at the moment, so I feel that it is wise to go over the plan in case there are any problems in it that we somehow missed in the planning stages. Then again, if there are any issues, it is almost certainly too late by now to go back and correct them.

Our ultimate goal is to defeat Reunification, that secretive organization which has the goal of 'reuniting' Dela and Xeeo. In order to learn more about how Reunification is progressing in their goal—which we know very little of due to having no spies within the organization to relay their plans to us—we have decided to kidnap the most well-known and high-profile member of Reunification: Mayor Xacron-Ah.

According to the Foundation, Xacron-Ah's primary job, from what they have gathered, is to keep non-members of Reunification from entering the Dead Lands and accidentally discovering Reunification's operations out there. He uses his authority as the Mayor to enforce laws preventing Xeeonite citizens and even foreigners from entering the Dead Lands.

Therefore, we believe that Xacron-Ah will be able to tell us quite a bit about Reunification. He has been seen in contact with the Leader of Reunification, a woman called Kiriah, which is a good sign that he will be able to offer us valuable intelligence if we can get him.

Our plan, then, is to break into the Mayor's Mansion—a building only a block away from our current position—kidnap Xacron-Ah, and then take him to our current base of operations, where we will then interrogate him for the information we need.

As for how we plan to do that, it is simple. Konoa will start a riot in the streets of Xeeon, which will force the majority of the J bots in the vicinity to try to contain it. While they are distracted by the rioting, Lanresia and I will go to the Mayor's Mansion and break through its security forces, kidnap Xacron-Ah himself, and then leave, hopefully before my fellow officers succeed in ending the riot and returning to check on the Mayor.

In fact, the whole reason I am even here is because I have detailed knowledge of the Mayor's Mansion. I have never served on Xacron-Ah's personal security force; however, the mobile Database stored in my memory contains a map of the Mayor's Mansion, as well as knowledge of the other security measures put in place to keep him safe. By using my knowledge, we should have little trouble breaking into the Mansion and kidnapping Xacron-Ah, assuming nothing goes wrong.

Even though I understand that this is all for the greater good, my programming makes me want to rebel against it. Defending Xacron-Ah's life is one of the few specific commands directly coded into our AI. We are not supposed to kidnap or hurt him in any way, because he is the Mayor, and the Mayor is considered an even higher authority than the Database among us J bots.

Furthermore, I find the idea of intentionally starting a riot to be legally questionable. As a J bot, it is my duty to stop or prevent riots from breaking out, not to be an accomplice to one. Under ordinary circumstances, I should arrest Konoa and Lanresia both and put them in the Xeeon City Prison, where they will await their trial in the courts.

But right now, I must put aside the law in order to protect it. Even I understand that it is more important to stop Reunification than it is to enforce the law. Besides, if I return to my fellow officers, I will likely be scrapped, as I was framed for the murders of several Knights, which makes me a liability for the J bots as a whole.

Yet when I look at the roof of the Mayor's Mansion—which

peeks out over one of the nearby buildings—I find it hard to resist my programming, which tells me to defend the building from those who want to kidnap him. It is a strong … not exactly a feeling, because we J bots do not have 'feelings' of any sort. It is a command, one that I find difficult to ignore, though I manage it nonetheless.

Lanresia, on the other hand, does not seems to be suffering from the internal strife I am. She only appears worried because she is afraid of my former fellow officers finding and arresting us. She has not told me that, but I can tell, because they are currently the only real threat to our plan.

I have no words of comfort for her, seeing as I do not know how to comfort someone. I consider telling another joke from *Secrets of Humor*, but then decide that it is better to keep silent and not accidentally draw the attention of the law enforcers to us with a joke that she will probably not even laugh at. That is the reason, as far as I can tell, why the Foundation agents I have met do not find my humor appealing; it is Xeeonite humor and they are Delanians, which means that their sense of humor is different from mine, although that does not help me find out exactly what they find humorous and what they don't.

Lanresia, peering around the side of the billboard again, suddenly gestures for me to look around with her. As silently as I can, I walk over to her side and peer around the billboard, though at first I do not understand what she wants me to look at.

Then I see Konoa standing on top of a parked hover vehicle. He is wearing a looser, hood-like skull mask to hide his identity, along with a pair of dark goggles over the eye holes, which I consider unnecessary because his face is not in the Database.

Then again, I suppose Konoa probably wishes to stay out of the Database as much as he can, so wearing a mask to hide his identity makes sense.

None of the Xeeonians in the streets appear to take notice of him at first, likely because he has not drawn attention to himself yet, although a handful of human teenagers point and snicker at his mask (they probably think it looks ridiculous). Even my fellow J bots do not stop to demand he show his ID, although that may be because he is not currently behaving in any illegal manner yet.

Then Konoa raises a large, round object in his hand: A blind bomb. I recall Konoa saying that he is going to use a blind bomb to start the confusion, so I am not surprised to see it. I do wonder where he found such a large one, however, considering most blind bombs are only large enough to fit inside the average human fist.

Lanresia's speaking snake uncurls from around her waist and rises up by her head. Its glowing eyes are looking at Konoa as it says, "Ready, J997?"

I nod and whisper, "Affirmative."

"All right," says Lanresia, her voice as low as mine. "I am going to send Konoa a message telling him to throw the blind bomb now. Just be ready to run for the Mansion as soon as it goes off."

"I am always ready," I say. "And do not worry about getting past Xacron-Ah's security systems; I will handle that when we get there."

"Good," says Lanresia. "Now I am sending this message to Konoa. Once he gets it, he will—"

Lanresia is interrupted when Konoa hefts the large blind bomb and tosses it directly into the center of the loud, busy streets of Xeeon. As soon as the blind bomb lands in the streets, it explodes, creating a massive blinding light that is immediately followed by the terrified and confused screams of the people.

I, however, am not blinded by the light, because I activate the darkening filters on my optics to prevent the blind bomb from damaging them. This allows me to see the J bots soaring from all around the nearby skyscrapers, trying to restore peace and order to the now confused mass of citizens running around and screaming in the streets below. I spot Konoa making a break for it, going in the opposite direction of the Mayor's Mansion, causing several officers to fly after him immediately. Smart move. It means my former fellow officers will be less likely to notice Lanresia and I as we make our way to the Mayor's Mansion.

Lanresia grabs onto my shoulders and I fly us both down to the alleyway between the building we stood on and the one next to it. As we touch the streets, I find it hard to ignore the screams and sounds of rioting in the streets behind us, but I focus my attention solely on our mission, which will matter more in the long run than stopping this riot.

Once Lanresia lets go of my shoulders, the two of us run down the alley, which is completely abandoned. There are not even any beggars here, which is good, because the fewer people who see us, the better.

In less than a minute, we arrive at the area behind the Mayor's Mansion. It is a large building—not quite as large as the skyscrapers that tower it, but large enough—that looks antiquated compared to the rest of the city, which makes sense, seeing as the Mayor's Mansion is older than the rest of Xeeon, having been built by the first settlers of this region fifty years ago or so. Removing my darkening filter (which is no longer necessary, thanks to the light from the blind bomb having gone away) allows me to see that the Mansion has a large dome rising from the center, while four turrets rise from every corner.

The Mayor's Mansion is surrounded by an electric fence on all sides. The electric fence is strong enough to knock out anyone who tries to touch it and can shorten out any electrical gadgets used on it. Even we J bots are not entirely immune from its effects, which is why I am careful to keep my distance.

I see none of my fellow J bots around, but Lanresia and I keep to the shadows anyway. The Mayor's Mansion has security cameras affixed to the outside, which means that it is impossible to enter without being seen. Even simply walking by the Mansion's fence unseen is impossible, because the security cameras are always on and constantly filming everyone and everything that comes near the Mansion's vicinity. If the cameras see us as we try to break into the Mansion, they will send an automated alert to Database to send officers to arrest us, and our entire plan will fall apart.

Other security hazards include motion sensors in the garden around the Mansion, as well as an electric grid running underneath the ground to electrocute any trespassers who somehow make it past the fence. It is quite the well-defended area.

But we are not going to climb or even fly over the fence. That will be too obvious and will ruin the plan before it even passes phase one.

Instead, I bend over and remove the manhole cover on the street near us. Lanresia wrinkles her nose when she looks down it, likely smelling the waste below (which I am unable to, as J bots are not designed with noses or the ability to smell anything). Still, she climbs down the ladder anyway, and I follow suit, pulling the cover over our heads as soon as we are both inside.

We are going down into the sewers because the Mayor's Mansion has a secret escape route connected to them. No one knows about this secret escape route outside of the Mayor himself and us J bots; in fact, even many of us J bots are ignorant of its existence. I only know of it because I was once chosen to protect the Mayor and given this information, but then it was decided that someone else would do a better job as a bodyguard than I would. I was allowed to keep the information in case of an emergency, although I am not quite sure that this is what the Database was thinking of when it told me that.

The files state that this secret escape route is only to be used if Xeeon is under attack and it is unsafe for the Mayor to escape above ground or if the Mansion's teleporters are broken. According to the files, the secret escape route leads to a teleporter that will take the Mayor out of Xeeon and to wherever he needs to go in order to be safe.

Lanresia reaches the bottom first. A couple of seconds later, I am standing by her and using my built-in night vision to look at our surroundings.

I have only been down in the sewers of Xeeon a handful of times, so I am not as familiar with their layout as I should have been. They are dark, with dirty water and waste flowing down the center from wherever they come from. I see turned-off lights on the walls, but I have no way to activate them. Lanresia and I stand on the raised edges of the sewers, which appear to go down quite a ways, although the exact length is irrelevant to the plan, so I don't think about it.

Lanresia looks quite sick, because her face is turning green and she has her hands over her stomach. Still, she is not complaining, although I wonder if her sickness might harm us. I hope not, but it is too late to send her back now and I do not have any medicine to help calm her stomach.

According to the mobile Database, we need to walk straight ahead. I lead this time, because I am the only one of us who has an idea of what to expect ahead. Lanresia follows me, but she is so light on her feet that even my advanced audio receptors do not always pick up the sounds of her footsteps.

I walk forward without any reservation, despite the darkness of the sewers. I do this because I know that the secret escape route has no security in it at all. No cameras, no J bots, nothing. This is due to its secrecy; because no one knows about it, the Mayor thought it is unnecessary to add extra security measures. That is why it will be easy for Lanresia and me to use this route; assuming all goes well, we should have the Mayor out of here with little trouble.

"J997?" says Lanresia behind me, her voice a whisper. "Did you hear that?"

I stop and look over my shoulder at Lanresia. Her pointed elvish ears are twitching, a sign that she is trying to hone in on a particular sound that she hears. Her facial expression is still quite sick, although she looks like she is trying to concentrate hard on whatever it is she is listening for.

"Hear what, Lanresia?" I ask. "My audio receptors do not pick up anything down here."

Lanresia frowns. "It sounded like claws scraping against brick. And … something swimming in the waste water."

I increase the volume of my audio receptors to see if I can hear that same sound. My audio receptors pick up nothing at first, but then I hear something swimming in the dirty water flowing through the center of the sewers. I peer at the water, but it is so thick with waste that I cannot see through it at all.

"What is it?" Lanresia asks, her voice more than a little worried.

"I cannot see it," I say. "It may simply be a sewer dweller, which is a type of lizard that exists in the sewers of Xeeon and other cities. They are usually harmless, content to swim in the dirty water and waste that flows down here, and do not care to attack anything that does not pose an immediate threat to them."

Lanresia sighs. "Oh, that's good. I thought it might be something worse."

"We have nothing to fear down here," I say, shaking my head and turning away from the waste water. "Nothing at all. The sewers are abandoned even by the city's homeless. No one ever comes down here, aside from sewage workers and maintenace crews, so I believe we will be just fine. We must continue going forward until we find the secret entrance to the Mayor's Mansion."

Lanresia nods, but then she looks at the wall to our right and jumps. "What is that?"

I look at what she has seen. The wall at first looks as slimy and greenish as the rest of the tunnel does, but upon further inspection, I see a dried coating of blood on the wall. Sensors indicate that it is human blood, although when I run a sample through the mobile Database, it does not match any known Xeeonian citizen's blood. This is probably due to the blood's age, as well as the bacteria of the sewer that has no doubt mixed with it.

But it is not just a little blood; it is a lot of blood. It is almost like a second coat of paint. That is indeed strange, but when I look around, I do not see any bodies that the blood could have come from, which makes me wonder where it came from.

"Why is there blood on the wall?" asks Lanresia. She looks like she wants to run, but to her credit, she does not. "What is going on down here?"

"I do not know for certain," I say. "There should not be any blood down here at all. To my knowledge, the only organic beings to have ever been down here were the original workers who built this sewer, but the Database does not record any of them dying."

"I don't like this," says Lanresia. "Let's just hurry on and find the—"

Lanresia is interrupted by the sound of water splashing behind us. I whirl around in time to see a large, humanoid-like lizard creature bursting from the waste water, its open maw revealing row upon row of deadly teeth, its sharp claws extended out before it.

Before I can react, the lizard humanoid grabs me and pulls me back into the waste water with it. I hear Lanresia scream behind me as that happens, but I am unable to respond and her scream is cut off the moment my head goes beneath the surface of the water.

In the waste water, I am unable to see anything due to the thick sewage and waste in my optics. Sensors indicate, however, that the lizard humanoid—which must be one of the same creatures that attacked the Foundation's Delanian and Xeeonite branches two and a half weeks ago—is holding me tight and biting at every part of my body it can get.

I try to fight back by punching and kicking at the creature, but my body is not designed to fight underwater; therefore, my attacks are weak and ineffective. The lizard humanoid, however, must have been designed to fight here, because it has no trouble at all attacking me through the thick sludge and waste all around us.

Its attacks do not hurt, but I doubt it will be long before it tears through my armor and succeeds in damaging my internals. Therefore, I must end this fight quickly and reunite with Lanresia; although my resolve to end this fight quickly does not make the lizard humanoid fight any less viciously.

But then I remember my electrical barrier, which, if I choose to activate it, will electrocute the lizard humanoid and probably kill it. But I hesitate to do us underwater, because it might end up short-circuiting me as well.

Instead, I activate my laser vision, firing twin beams at the lizard humanoid biting at me. My lasers strike it in the neck, causing the lizard humanoid to let go of me in response. I then kick at it as hard as I can, making contact with its chest, and then activate my boosters to allow me to rocket out of the water quickly.

RETALIATION

Bursting through the surface of the waste water, I almost fly into the low ceiling of the escape tunnel before I succeed in stopping myself. Then I hear Lanresia's cry and look to my right to see what is happening to her.

She is surrounded on both sides by a couple of lizard humanoids, although the creatures are keeping their distance from her because she is firing her laser gun at them. She does not hit them, probably because her fear is affecting her aim, but so far she does not appear wounded by them, which is good.

I aim my eye lasers at them, but before I can fire, there is splash below and the lizard humanoid I fought in the waste water below bursts out and grabs onto my ankles. The sudden change in weight throws off my balance and almost causes me to be dragged down back into the water.

But then I put more power into my boosters, sending out large flames that burn the lizard humanoid's hands. It roars in pain and lets go, falling back into the water with a splash, while I regain my balance and look at Lanresia's situation again.

She fires her laser gun at the lizard humanoids, but her aim is poor, likely due to her fear and the darkness overriding her rational senses. The lizard humanoids have no trouble dodging her blasts and are about to attack her, prompting me to fly down toward her as fast as I can.

I land on the concrete floor and then lash out with a kick aimed at one of the lizard humanoids. My foot connects with its jaw, sending it staggering backward from the impact, and then I follow it up with a laser blast from my eyes, striking it in the heart. My lasers cut a black, bloody hole in its chest, causing the lizard humanoid to collapse onto the floor instantly.

Then I turn my attention to the second one, which is standing back as if to analyze me. Lanresia, who is behind me, points her laser gun at it, but before she can pull the trigger and shoot, the lizard humanoid opens its mouth and unleashes a stream of fire at us.

I knock Lanresia down and then step forward to take the brunt of the blast. The flames bathe over me, but I do not feel the heat. However, my internal thermometer says that my temperature is rapidly rising, even with my external cooling shields activating to prevent my exterior from being melted. Even so, the flames are hot enough that I know I must end this quickly before they break through my cooling shields and cause serious damage to my exterior.

The flames obscure my optics, but I can guess where the lizard humanoid is easily. I fire twin lasers at it, hear the lasers sizzle against its skin, and then the flames abruptly cut off. At the same time, my exterior temperature rapidly returns to normal, while the lizard humanoid that had been trying to kill me falls dead on the floor. My lasers appear to have gone through its open mouth, which likely means that they hit its brain.

In any case, these two lizard humanoids are dead, but I still sense the third one in the waste water below. I hesitate to go after it, however, because I know how deadly that creature can fight in the water.

Just as I think that, the lizard humanoid splashes out from the water again, roaring like a Great Lizard as it lunges toward me. Without hesitation, I raise my hand and fire a single finger lightning bolt at the creature.

The finger lightning bolt strikes it in the chest, causing it to roar in pain as it is electrocuted. It falls back into the water, splashing up more waste as it does so, but this time, my sensors pick up no signs of life below. That final lightning bolt likely did the trick.

I turn to Lanresia. She is panting hard and looking sicker and more frightened than ever, even though all signs indicate that we are currently safe from any other unexpected threats.

"Those monsters are down here?" says Lanresia, still holding her gun as if the battle is not over. "You said that there weren't any guards down here. Why—"

"I admit to being wrong about that, but the explanation is quite logical," I say. "The lizard humanoids work for Reunification. Most likely, Xacron-Ah placed them down here in order to more effectively protect himself from possible intruders. I doubt he thought anyone would actually come this way, but he obviously wanted to be safer than sorry."

Lanresia's eyes flick to the blood-stained wall. "What about the blood, then?"

"I do not know," I say. "Perhaps someone else came down here—likely a sewer worker, seeing as this is still part of the sewers and no one else knows about this place—and the lizard humanoids attacked and killed him under the mistaken belief that he was a threat to Xacron-Ah's life."

As I say that, a hat floats by us on the waste water. It appears to me to be the cap usually worn by Xeeon sewer workers, although it is so covered in grime and waste that I cannot tell for sure.

Lanresia shivers. "Those things are so horrible. Just awful."

I nod. "They are indeed quite terrifying, but there is no reason

189

for us to be afraid. They are all dead, and it is unlikely that there are any more down here, because I doubt Xacron-Ah thought he needed more than that."

Lanresia holds her gun close to her chest, however. "Maybe, but I'm going to keep my gun out anyway."

Because I do not expect us to get into any more fights, I find her desire to keep her gun un-holstered rather odd.

I am about to comment on it before I remember that Lanresia has already had terrible experiences with these creatures. She is one of the few survivors of Reunification's assault on the Foundation's Xeeonite branch and is also a survivor of Reunification's attack on the Foundation's Delanian branch. She may even be suffering from some kind of stress disorder, although I again say nothing about it, because aside from this odd (yet understandable) action of hers, she seems to be functioning as normally as ever. Still, I resolve to keep a closer eye on her in case the stress of the situation causes her to break down, however unlikely that may seem at the moemnt.

With the lizard humanoids out of the way, it only takes us a few more minutes of walking to find the secret ladder leading up to the Mayor's Mansion. The ladder is hidden behind a portion of the concrete wall that resembles every other part of the wall; however, my keen optics spy a cracked part of the wall which resembles a panel. I press my hand against it and the wall slides away, revealing a rather simple metal ladder leading up into the shadows above.

This time, I go first, because I am better able to handle whatever may await us above than Lanresia is. I doubt we will run into any real problems, however, because this ladder should take us directly to Xacron-Ah's bedroom. Knowing the Mayor's schedule, he should be either asleep or about to go to sleep at this very moment. Xacron-Ah always sleeps alone in his room, so we probably will not run into any guards. Of course, he usually has his bodyguards stationed outside his room, so Lanresia and I will need to be as silent as the Dead Lands once we get there.

It takes us only a couple of minutes of climbing to reach the hatch leading into Xacron-Ah's room. The hatch is normally locked, but I know the secret combination to undo it.

Unfortunately, the hatch is locked from the outside. It is designed to allow someone to *leave* Xacron-Ah's room, not enter it via the sewers. That is why it cannot be unlocked from the inside

Even this problem is not as insurmountable as it first appears, however. A quick but careful application of my laser vision destroys the lock and allows me to lift it.

But I do not throw the hatch open; instead, I carefully raise it inch by inch. While I doubt Xacron-Ah will notice, seeing as this hatch is carefully hidden in his room, I cannot risk him noticing us before he needs to.

As I lift the hatch, I gradually gain a better view of the room it is in. It is a dark room, not very large, without any lights or any furniture in it. There is a door directly in front of us, however, which should lead us into his closet, which will then lead us into his actual room.

Seeing no one here, I lift the hatch all the way open and climb out. Lanresia follows me and looks happy that we are no longer down there. She still does not holster her gun, however, and when she looks at me, she wrinkles her nose again.

"You smell awful," says Lanresia in a whisper. "Must be the sewage water."

"I do not think it matters," I say. "I can still kidnap Xacron-Ah whether I smell good or bad."

"What if he smells you before we sneak up on him?" says Lanresia. She pinches her nose. "Because when I say you smell awful, I mean *awful*."

"I have no way of cleaning myself off," I say. "But I wonder if your concealment ring can also hide scents."

Lanresia glances at the skyras ring on her finger and says, "I think so, but that requires more skyras usage than normal. I may not be able to maintain it for long."

"You do not need to," I say. "All you need to do is maintain it for a few minutes. That is all the time we will need to kidnap Xacron-Ah."

"If you say so," says Lanresia. "You seem pretty confident about our ability to kidnap him."

"I know neither confidence nor doubt," I say. "As a robot, I know only that I must do what I must do."

"Right," says Lanresia, who has a hint of doubt in her voice. "Well, let's just get going. There's no telling how much time we have before the J bots get that crowd under control and return to their original positions, which will make it harder for us to escape with Xacron-Ah once we catch him."

I nod and walk over to the door in front of us. It is unlocked, allow me to wave my hand and cause the door to slide open. I find that odd, because I expected it to be locked. Then again, if Xacron-Ah ever needs to make a quick escape, it is probably more practical for him to keep this door unlocked than locked.

RETALIATION

When Lanresia and I step through the doorway, we find ourselves hidden behind rows of large suits, equally-large shirts, and other clothing. The mobile Database says that Xacron-Ah's secret escape route is hidden within his closet, which explains the presence of so many suits hanging in front of us.

Based on the darkness of the closet, the door must be closed; however, when I push aside some of the suits (thus getting some of the waste water on them, although that is unimportant at the moment), I see that the closet door is in fact cracked open just slightly. It appears that Xacron-Ah has failed to close the door for some reason. Then again, I recall that Xacron-Ah is well-known for his sloppiness in minor matters such as this, so this is not surprising.

Still, Lanresia and I push aside his suits as quietly as we can. I do not know if Xacron-Ah is in fact in his room yet or if he is even awake. All I know is that we must be careful nonetheless; this entire plan hinges on our kidnapping Xacron-Ah. If we fail at right now, it is highly unlikely we will get an opportunity to try this again.

As it turns out, however, Xacron-Ah's closet has more than merely clothes in it. We step over old, forgotten pairs of shoes, cardboard boxes containing objects we cannot see, and other articles of clothing, such as ties and socks. Once we even find a tiny metal ball that hums when you touch it, but thankfully we learn how to turn it off and do so before it can alert Xacron-Ah's attention to his closet.

As we walk closer to the door, I see blue lights flashing through the crack, as well as voices that sound like they are deep in conversation. One of them is Xacron-Ah's deep, rumbling voice; the other is unfamiliar, although if Xacron-Ah's tone is a clue, he is clearly someone with authority over the Mayor.

Enhancing my audio receptors, I listen hard to Xacron-Ah's conversation, gesturing at Lanresia to stop so I can hear him more clearly.

"... yes, Founder, of course," says Xacron-Ah. He sounds worn out, but he is clearly making an effort to hide it. "No, we have had no luck in locating that rogue J bot on Dela. I've been working with Kalcan to find him, but Kalcan says that he can't find him anywhere. On the plus side, we've moved more shipments of super speed from Dela to Xeeo in the past couple of days than we did in all of last month."

I look at Lanresia, who must have heard Xacron-Ah as well, because she is now staring at me in surprise. It is obvious to us both that Xacron-Ah is talking about me, unless there happens to be another 'rogue' J bot somewhere on Dela who is also working against Reunification that I do not know of.

Even more interesting, however, is his reference to someone with the title 'Founder.' That title can only belong to the mysterious and enigmatic head of Reunification, which means that Xacron-Ah is speaking with him right now. If so, then I may be able to get my first glimpse of the Founder.

Gesturing for Lanresia to stay still, I make my way to the cracked door, still listening to the conversation all the while.

"You better find him quick," says the unfamiliar voice, which I believe belongs to the Founder. "I do not appreciate having someone outside of our organization knowing about us and our plans. It is only a matter of time before he reconnects with the authorities and reveals our existence to them. And I do not care

194

about the drugs, despite the role they will play in the completion of the Mission."

"Yes, Founder, I understand," says Xacron-Ah. "But don't worry. If that J bot ever steps back on Xeeo and tries to reconnect with the Database, I will be the first to know, and he will be reprogrammed and his memory wiped entirely, if not scrapped outright."

That does not alarm me, mostly because my lack of emotion makes it hard for me to feel alarmed at anything. Nonetheless, I hear the sincerity in Xacron-Ah's voice, which tells me he fully intends on carrying out that promise should he ever get his hands on me.

Reaching the door, I peer through the crack as carefully as I can, adjusting my optics to see better in the darkness of Xacron-Ah's room.

Due to the thinness of the crack, I cannot see much; however, I can see Xacron-Ah's massive back to me. He appears to be wearing his navy blue suit; unusual, seeing as he is by himself. Then again, it is highly likely that Xacron-Ah is awake because he just returned from an important political meeting of some sort.

Due to Xacron-Ah's bulk, I it is hard for me to see the Founder, who is a glowing blue hologram projecting in front of Xacron-Ah. I catch a glimpse of a head that appears half-organic, half-mechanical, which seems unusual; however, I see nothing else besides that.

"I hope so," says the Founder. "It would be … not good for us if this robot allied with the remnants of the Foundation. I am not afraid of a simple machine; however, I do worry about the Foundation."

"You don't need to worry about anything, Founder," says Xacron-Ah. "The Foundation is gone. Its twin bases on Xeeo and Dela are destroyed, most of its members are dead, and those few who survived both assaults are scattered and on the run. I even succeeded in having my J bots arrest a few of them, including Kojama himself."

A tiny, slightly metallic gasp behind me makes me look over my shoulder briefly. Lanresia is standing near me, having somehow moved close to me without me noticing. She looks shocked and terrified, which puzzles me, as I do not know who this 'Kojama' fellow is.

"Kojama?" says the Founder. His tone becomes softer. "Interesting. When will you execute him?"

"His execution is set for tomorrow," says Xacron-Ah, who sounds proud of himself. "It's going to be a spectacle for the whole city. Remember the Jaws massacre that happened a few weeks back?"

"I recollect you telling me about that sometime ago," says the Founder. "Was not the regretful day when a mad man entered the area of Xeeon known as 'the Jaws' and killed ten Rathonian immigrants, including three children?"

"Yes," says Xacron-Ah, nodding his large head, making his dreads fly around. "The J bots did not arrive in time to stop him. The killer is still on the loose; however, I am blaming Kojama for the murders that shocked the city. Since no one knows what the killer's face actually looks like, no one is questioning whether he is indeed the killer or not."

"Wise move," says the Founder. "You not only get to behead one of the Foundation's most important members in public, but you also get to do it without alerting the public to either organization's existence. Well done, Xacron-Ah, well done."

"All for the Mission, Founder," says Xacron-Ah. "I believe as you do, that anyone who stands in our way must die."

"That is the truest thing you have said in a long time," says the Founder. "Now I must let you know that we are closer than ever to completing the Mission. Indeed, I speculate it will only take us a few more days to do so, due to our rapid progress."

"Wonderful to hear, Found—" says Xacron-Ah, before the Founder interrupts him.

"Which is why I am speaking with you so early in the morning," says the Founder. His tone becomes harsher. "With the Mission so close to completion at this point, we cannot afford even the most minor of mistakes. Do you hear me?"

Xacron-Ah steps back, even though the Founder is merely a hologram that cannot hurt him. "Why, er, yes, Founder, I understand completely. I have done my best in everything that I do. I would never make a mistake that could cost us the entire Mission."

"I know how eagerly you believe that," says the Founder. "But I must repeat it: *Do not make any mistakes*. If you slip up even once, when we are so close to healing the worlds, I will know about it, and you will not live long enough to repeat it."

Xacron-Ah runs his hand through his locks. "Yes, sir, I understa—"

"You are not important," the Founder interrupts again. "Remember that your life is insignificant in the long run. You are not so important that I will hesitate to snuff out your insignificant life if you mess up. Every step you take, you take on the narrow road, with death awaiting to embrace you on either side of the deep, dark pit you walk over."

"Yes, sir, of cou—"

"Good," says the Founder. "Now I believe we have covered everything. I must now go and return to my chambers. As for you, make no mistakes, do not attract any unnecessary attention to yourself, and use whatever force necessary to subdue our enemies."

Xacron-Ah bows deeply, allowing me a glimpse of the holographic Founder. He wears golden wizard robes and has a half-organic, half-mechanical face. Not entirely unusual, seeing as many Xeeonites have 'two faces,' as that feature is called, but the Founder's face does not look like typical two faces.

Then Xacron-Ah rises to his full height again and the Founder is gone from my view once more. "Yes, Founder sir. I understand. Glory be to the Mission!"

"Indeed," says the Founder. "If anything comes up, contact Kiriah immediately. At this point, I cannot be distracted by anything less than the most urgent of emergencies. Understood?"

"Yes, Founder sir," says Xacron-Ah. "I will make certain of it."

"Very well," says the Founder. "Assuming all goes well, the next time we see each other, it will be on the healed world, where all is one."

Then the Founder's hologram vanished. As soon as it did, Xacron-Ah gasped and staggered back. He put a hand on his forehead, but with his back to us, I cannot see his face. However, my sensors indicate that his blood pressure is rising fast.

"Oh god," says Xacron-Ah, panting as though he has run a

mile. "Oh god, oh god, how did I get into this? Why, why, why."

His sudden fear makes me look at Lanresia. She, however, appears to be thinking about this 'Kojama' person, whoever he is, to notice.

I turn my attention to the crack in the door, watching as Xacron-Ah begins pacing back and forth across his room, disappearing and reappearing in my view every now and then.

"This is deeper than I've ever been in before," says Xacron-Ah. He appears to be talking to himself. "I was promised riches and fame and I got that, but god does that man scare me. I'm not even sure he's a man. Just what the hell is he, anyway? Some kind of immortal monster, that's what he is."

He appears to be talking about the Founder, which puzzles me. He must not be as loyal to the Founder or to Reunification as he appears.

Xacron-Ah stops and begins pulling at his locks, which I recognize as one of his nervous habits. "Thinks he can boss me around and threaten me. *Me*, Xacron-Ah, Mayor of Xeeon, best former super speed dealer in the world. And then he just blows off the good news about how our shipments are coming along. What the hell. Who does he think he is?"

I hear Lanresia moving a little bit closer. She seems to be listening to Xacron-Ah's rambling as well.

Then Xacron-Ah falls to his knees and hides his face in his hands. "Oh god, what if he heard me say that? Of course, he probably didn't. My communicator is off and the room isn't bugged. I made sure of that. No, he can't hear me. Bastard can't hear me at all."

Then Xacron-Ah is up and pacing again. "About the only

good thing that idiot's done for me is help me win this office. Even then, being Mayor isn't all that great. Endless meetings, political scheming among the members of Parliament, stupid people demanding I support this or that law … sometimes, I think this is a horrible nightmare that will end if I would only just wake the *hell* up."

It appears to me that Xacron-Ah must have some kind of mental condition. Possibly the stress of the job is getting to him, although I do not recall ever hearing from the others about this side of the Mayor.

Then Xacron-Ah stops and stomps his foot on the floor without warning. "Just brushing off my report about the drugs … doesn't he realize that this wouldn't be possible if I wasn't in charge of the city? He's the one who harped on and on and on and *on* to me about the importance of these drugs in distracting the J bots and the general population from the *real* issues, but now he's acting like it's as trivial as a child's toy? What an idiot."

Now that is a particular piece of information I had not known. It is true that smuggling and usage of super speed drugs among the population of Xeeon and its surrounding countryside and cities has increased tenfold; however, I did not know that it is because of Xacron-Ah's aid. That certainly explains why Reunification hired a former drug dealer to lead the city.

"I can't handle this," says Xacron-Ah. He licks his lips and looks at something over his shoulder, out of sight. "I need my hit. I need it. Gotta calm down. Can't sleep if I'm worried about everything. Nope. Can't."

He walks out of my line of sight. Then I hear a drawer open, followed by it closing again. Next, I hear Xacron-Ah sitting down on what sounds like a chair and then a low moan of pleasure that I have little trouble recognizing as the moan of an individual who is injecting super speed into his body.

I look at Lanresia. Her hands are covering her mouth; her organic mouth, that is. Her speaking snake's mouth is unobstructed, but it does not appear to be about to speak.

"Think we should get him now?" says Lanresia, her voice a low whisper, although thanks to my enhanced audio receptors, I still hear her well.

"Wait," I whisper in return, holding up one hand. "Just wait. Let us wait until Xacron-Ah is too drugged to fight back."

Lanresia frowns, but nods. "Okay."

Of course, I do not know how long it will take for Xacron-Ah to do so. Depending on how used his body is to the drug, he might take anywhere from five minutes to several hours before he is knocked out by the drugs. His fatigue should help, however, because it is a well-known fact about super speed that people become higher on it the more tired they are.

We stand in his closet, listening closely to Xacron-Ah's moans of pleasure. He seems to have a high tolerance for the drug, because he still sounds like he is aware. This does not surprise me, however, because due to his past as a dealer of the drug, Xacron-Ah's body likely has developed a tolerance for the drug, despite its destructive effects on the human body. Again, the mobile Database does not mention Xacron-Ah having a history of drug usage, but at this point, I expected that, as the mobile Database does not seem to have any useful information on anything anymore.

Then—without warning—a loud *thump* breaks the monotony.

Lanresia and I continue to stand here, however, and listen for a couple of more minutes for Xacron-Ah to continue moaning; instead, we begin to hear him snoring loudly.

With a nod at Lanresia, I carefully but quickly push open the closet door. It opens softly against the carpeted floor, making virtually no noise. Once it is open completely, Lanresia and I step into Xacron-Ah's room.

This is the first time I have stepped foot in this place, because we J bots—even Xacron-Ah's bodyguards—are not allowed in here. Therefore, I look around at the room in order to commit it to my memory.

It is a large, wide-open room, almost taking up the entire floor that it is on. The floor has soft elfish carpeting, while the walls have fine oak wood paneling. An entertainment center, with a large black sofa and a hologram projector, takes up the center of the room, while the door to the bathroom is opened slightly on the other side of the room.

Xacron-Ah's bed is about a dozen feet away from us. It is a large bed, appropriate for a man of his size, with red drapes surrounding it. It looks more Delanian than Xeeonite, which makes sense, seeing as Xacron-Ah is a native of Dela and not Xeeo.

But Xacron-Ah is not sleeping on his bed. The Mayor is instead lying on the floor next to his bed, snoring loudly, his arms splayed out. In his right hand is a needle full of the green liquid known as super speed, although 'full' is not the most correct word. It is half-full at best, although that is still far too much super speed for one human to inject into himself.

In front of Xacron-Ah is a chest of drawers. The top chest is open, which is no doubt where he kept the needle. I consider digging around inside it to find out what else Xacron-Ah is hiding from us, but then I remember that we have very little time as is and that we need to spend most of that time dragging Xacron-Ah out of here.

Lanresia and I walk up to the unconscious Xacron-Ah, who, aside from his snoring, is not moving at all. I remove the super speed needle from his hand and toss it into the nearest trash can. Then Lanresia and I grab his arms and begin dragging him toward his closet.

Xacron-Ah is a large, heavy man; however, we J bots can lift up to two tons of metal, so dragging him along is not much of a challenge for me. Lanresia, on the other hand, appears to be putting her all into helping. I consider telling her that she does not need to and that I can drag and even carry Xacron-Ah all on my own, but as we are trying to be as quiet as possible, I decide not to mention it.

We have little trouble carrying Xacron-Ah through the open doorway of his closet; however, just to be safe, I close it when we get inside. I doubt anyone will be checking on Xacron-Ah until the morning, by which time we will be long gone; however, I do not want to take any chances.

Kicking aside shoes and other assorted items on the floor of Xacron-Ah's closet, we make our way to the back, where the door to the secret escape route is still open. I find it interesting how close we are to escaping without anyone noticing, but I keep my mouth shut. While I am not superstitious at all, even I have noticed a times how easy it is to 'jinx' oneself, as the Delanians tend to put it.

Considering how important this mission is, I cannot afford to 'jinx' either of us.

When we arrive at the hatch, this is where we meet our first real obstacle. While Xacron-Ah is still sleeping and snoring as soundly as ever, we do not seem to have any easy way to transport Xacron-Ah down it. His bulk should fit through, seeing as the hatch is wide; however, I do not know if I can carry him down myself.

Turning to Lanresia, I ask, "Do you have any idea how we can transport Xacron-Ah down the hatch?"

Lanresia strokes her chin. "We need some sort of platform we could lower him down on."

I look around the dark, furniture-less room. "I do not see any platform on hand or even any rope or cables we could use to lower him down with."

Lanresia shrugs. "Then I don't know how we can move him out of here. Unless you think you can hold him over your shoulder while climb down at the same time?"

I shake my head. "Negative. While I do have the strength necessary to lift up Xacron-Ah, trying to climb down the ladder while supporting him on my shoulder at the same time is impossible."

"I knew it," says Lanresia. She looks at Xacron-Ah in worry. "Then how do we get him out of here? It's not like we can just take the elevator."

I consider the problem logically for a few seconds before a possible solution occurs to me when I glance at the unconscious Xacron-Ah. "I have an idea."

"What is it?" says Lanresia.

"I will show it to you," I say. "Stand back and watch."

Lanresia does as I ask, giving me some room to move. I bend over Xacron-Ah, who is still snoring without end, and shake him gently as I say, in a low voice, "Mayor Xacron-Ah, please wake up. Can you hear me, Mayor Xacron-Ah?"

Lanresia immediately grabs my shoulder. I look over my shoulder at her and see an alarmed look on both of her faces.

"What the hell do you think you're doing?" says Lanresia, her voice still little more than a whisper. "If you wake him up, he'll call in his guards, and the whole plan will be ruined."

"I understand your concerns, Lanresia, but please do not worry," I say, shrugging off her hand. "I know what I am doing. We will not be caught and Xacron-Ah will certainly not call in his bodyguards. Of that, I can assure you."

Lanresia's faces look at me skeptically, but then she steps back and folds her arms across her shoulder. She does not look away, however; instead, she focuses on me with a look that is quite clearly disapproving of my plan, even though she does not yet know what it is.

Turning back to face Xacron-Ah, I gently shake him again, saying, "Mister Mayor, are you wake?"

Then Xacron-Ah's snoring ceases and his eyes flicker open. He looks at me, but I can already tell that the super speed has destroyed his comprehension. His pupils are smaller and his eyes are bloodshot already, while his breath is unsteady.

"Huh?" says Xacron-Ah, staring at me with blank eyes I recognize from many arrests of super speed dealers. "What are you? Where am I?"

"Mister Mayor, you are on your way to a very important

meeting with the Xeeon Parliament," I say. "I am waking you up to get you ready to go. It's starting in ten minutes."

Xacron-Ah makes a dismissive grunt and says, "Bah. Those Parliament idiots can jump into the volcanic pits for all I care. Wake me for something important."

Xacron-Ah tries to close his eyes, but I shake him again, causing him to snap, "What is it now?"

"Sir, you have an important date with Kiriah," I say. "It is in ten minutes and I—"

Xacron-Ah sits up so quickly that he almost knocks his head into mine. He looks around wildly and says, "I have a date with her? Where? What time is it? Am I dressed and ready to go?"

I look at Lanresia, who is staring at me in sheer disbelief.

Then I look at Xacron-Ah and gesture at the hatch behind him. "Sir, we can reach the date quickly if we climb down this hatch into the sewers. It is a short cut to the place you agreed to meet her at."

Xacron-Ah staggers to his feet and almost falls into the hatch headfirst before regaining his balance. He then brushes his locks back and says, "How do I look? Do I look good?"

"Perfect, sir," I say. "Now we must leave soon, because Kiriah is waiting."

"Yes, yes, I agree," says Xacron-Ah, nodding. He pats the lip of the hatch. "Down this hatch, right?"

"Right," I say. I gesture at the ladder. "Just watch your step, because it is a long way down and if you fall on your head, that would force you to push back the date again."

"Again?" says Xacron-Ah, staring at me in alarm. "You mean I've missed my date with her before?"

"Yes," I say with as much sincerity as I can. "Several times, in fact. That is why we must hurry; in fact, that is why you told me to wake you up in time for your date today."

"Of course, of course," says Xacron-Ah. "Thank you so much. I should give you a raise and a promotion for all your hard work."

"It is nothing," I say, ignoring Lanresia's continual disbelieving stare. "I am only doing what any good servant would do in my situation."

"Very well," says Xacron-Ah. "I'll just climb down this ladder, then."

"I will come with you," I say. "You might not remember the date's location, so I will lead you there."

"Thanks," says Xacron-Ah. "You're a lifesaver. I don't know how I can repay you."

"Again, it is nothing," I say. "Now we must hurry, before Kiriah decides you are not going to show up and leaves."

Xacron-Ah nods and climbs down the ladder far more quickly than a man of his bulk should have been able to. I am about to follow when Lanresia says, "How did you do that?"

I look at Lanresia, who still has her arms folded across her chest. She is looking at me with extreme skepticism, as if I just performed some kind of magic trick that she cannot figure out on her own.

So I say, "One of the effects of super speed over usage is heightened susceptibility. I can effectively make Xacron-Ah do whatever I want simply by suggesting it to him."

Lanresia shakes her head in amazement. "Why didn't I think of that?"

"I've dealt with super speed dealers and users dozens of times before," I say. "It's how I learned about it. Now come on. If we let Xacron-Ah get too far ahead of us, we will lose him."

-

Retaliation is now available in ebook and trade paperback formats wherever books are sold!

About the Author

Timothy L. Cerepaka writes fantasy and science-fiction stories as an indie author. He is the author of the Prince Malock World fantasy novels, the Mages of Martir fantasy novels, and the science-fantasy standalone *The Last Legend: Glitch Apocalypse*. He lives in Texas.

Read about his other books at www.timothylcerepaka.com.

Other books by

Timothy L. Cerepaka

Prince Malock World:

The Mad Voyage of Prince Malock

The Return of Prince Malock

The New Era of Prince Malock

The Coronation of Prince Malock

Mages of Martir:

The Mage's Grave

The Mage's Limits

The Mage's Sea

The Mage's Ghost

Two Worlds:

Reunification

Alliance

Allegiance

Retaliation

Standalones:

The Last Legend: Glitch Apocalypse

All of the above novels are available in ebook and trade paperback wherever books are sold!

www.ingramcontent.com/pod-product-compliance
Lightning Source LLC
Chambersburg PA
CBHW061151170626
46809CB00003B/1053